Q'S Q: AN ARBOREAL NARRATIVE

mac wellman

Q's Q:

an Arboreal Narrative

GREEN INTEGER
KØBENHAVN & LOS ANGELES
2006

GREEN INTEGER BOOKS
Edited by Per Bregne
København / Los Angeles

Distributed in the United States by Consortium Book
Sales and Distribution, 1045 Westgate Drive, Suite 90
Saint Paul, Minnesota 55114-1065
Distributed in England and throughout Europe by
Turnaround Publisher Services
Unit 3, Olympia Trading Estate
Coburg Road, Wood Green, London N22 6TZ
44 (0)20 88293009

(323) 857-1115 / http://www.greeninteger.com

First Green Integer Edition 2006
©2006 by Mac Wellman
Back cover copy ©2006 by Green Integer
All rights reserved.

The author would like to thank the Yaddo and the MacDowell colonies
for stays which allowed for the writing of this fiction.
This book was made possible, in part, through a generous grant
from the Harold and Alma White Memorial Fund.

Design: Per Bregne
Typography: Kim Silva
Photograph of Mac Wellman

LIBRARY OF CONGRESS CATALOGING IN PUBLICATION DATA
Mac Wellman [1945]
Q's Q: An Arboreal Narrative
ISBN: 1-933382-51-1
p. cm – Green Integer 133
I. Title II. Series

Green Integer books are published for Douglas Messerli
Printed in the United States on acid-free paper.

Only the wicked walk in circles.

—ST AUGUSTINE

Names are Fates.

—PSEUDO MENNIPUS

I: Wolf

1: [THE NAME OF THE WOLF]

I propose to tell you about the time I became a wolf. In the world's eye, for I am not one, although "Wolfe" is my middle name: Wolfe with an "e" appended. I am called Christian W. Name, where double-u stands for you know what. C. W. Name. I would say "named"; but it would hardly do to write "my name is…Name." This rotation of reverie has occupied me a lot lately, even early this afternoon, as I drove down Route 8, the same old serpentine dither of a road, through Sweet Thumb's autumnal splendor to get here, where I am barricaded, behind twelve feet of concrete and high-carbon steel, in fortelleze. So I propose to tell you about how I first became a wolf because you will not believe me in any case, and secondly if I am going to be nailed for malfeasance I would prefer to be charged with an excess, not an economy of truth.

I hope someone will come to understand my situation for what it is, most dire. Before we end the intimation of were-craft let it be said that being an innocent charged with wolfishness has already tarnished my Christian name. I am no braggart. But I am no Proteus either, no chameleon. What I am presenting is no idle show, no Machiavellian stratagem, no act of wanton exhibitionism. I am just an ordinary guy; I am as I am; what you see is what you get, et cetera.

Q's Q, The play of which this soliloquy is but merely the merest detail possesses, as yet, no name in the conventional sense but as you may have already perceived Name has already nailed his fix upon it, focussed with great intensity his inner eye's wit, with a startling, staring, almost starling intensity. For I am in my distress, not merely Chris Name, an unknown playwright whose most recent extravaganza nearly caused a riot; but of that latter when I have established the architecture of my scene, or rather, my palpable disaster. For I am in my distress not merely Chris Name, but an Everyname: a lunar wolf sandwiched between two totally human words, words by which an entity is specified. The species of me; ergo, ego, the stuff of my representation. In brief, I am one of our perennially promising play-wrights; whose works may be seen on the second stages of theaters in Paris, Athens and Rome and in especial, Chenango and Palmyra where the aforementioned drama caused such a brouhaha. As for myself, all I recall of the incident in question is driving home propelled by a feeling of great, purring serenity; the horror of the actual fiasco eclipsed by my inner child's need to find solace, renewal and rebirth. Hope, that scarecrow.

The reading did not go well, did not go well indeed. So I seek release in natural things: Autumn has speckled the green bower of the whole county of Sweet Thumb. Russet, ruby and gold particulate matter rises and sinks, spiralling up and down amidst branches, boulders and worm-fences; swaying layers of maple, birch and oak spray; the staired fields, somber hedges and steep slate banks of the Sweet Thumb river valley, a geographical anomaly just west of Paris, Athens and Rome. Just north of the low, worked-out rustbelt plateau of Cairo, and Whitlow; where my daddy went broke in the drygoods business, and took to drink and the bitterness of univocal colloquy. Just west of Paris, Athens and Rome, as I prefer to imagine it; where golden apples ripen in a rich torus of orchard-land, just beyond the black shales of Wormwood; and here, where I am writing these words, with a bic pen on the reverse of some crumpled computer printout, alone, in the monitor room, where I am not supposed to be: in the Sweet Thumb Reactor complex nestled in its quiet little nook, a nook of a hook on the Sweet Thumb river near the Falls. I know Puella will ditch me in any case, after all this; the reading did not go well, did not go well at all; the roar of the crowd—like that of a great, malevolent beast!—that will stay with me for some time. Puella, Puella, the only Name you care for is your own.

The day before the reading, I had been in Palmyra buying painted shoes, for the reading of course, when it occurred to me, apropos of Puella, that adoration is selective. And not only is it selective, it is intransitive. The hot radiance of True Love flows not back to its quenchless source. Adoration is exacting since not only is it selective, it involves the divine issue of selection, which the Puritans among us know did not go out with real damnation and other haunts. I am not a Christian despite my name, but I do know adoration as a passion involves divine election, and for the chosen, bliss. Those truly chosen.

My own fate seems of a wholly other kind.

So, after the roar of my own undoing had washed over me and receded, as all bad things do, cross my heart; I sat in the parking lot and reflected. Reflected as I do now, as I load and unload my Smith and Wesson. Indian summer has lingered long past normal and sweetly so. It has fingered grasses and the sad, matted weed of what willows are: iridescent, leafy, beached seaweed hung out to dry. Airborne; as though adoration of willow were a soft wind smelling of pine and banks of phlox, wisteria and snapdragons.

Indeed, isn't "wolf" all our middles names?

2: [A PALMYRAN MEROPIA]

It was my first play, *Fishhead,* that caused all the trouble. I had submitted an early draft to the ten-minute play contest sponsored by the Ophidian Review, in nearby Whitlow. One of the judges was one Puella Carpenter. And it was she who wrote to notify me. Phrases such as "...exceptional promise...," "...deep emotional and pycho-sexual undertow..." tantalized my innocent's imagination; while others, such as "...a certain structural incoherence..." and "...a startling insensitivity to the plight of the social victim..." I found troubling. But all in all the tone of the letter was so upbeat and enthusiastic I was sure my theatrical career was safely christened. Puella requested copies of my previous scripts, which both delighted and frustrated me, since there were none. We agreed to meet at the Diner in Palmyra to discuss my promising future.

Puella proved demure, determined and slightly waxy-skinned, as if she had stood for too long near a fireplace, and had commenced to melt, slightly. Her eyes were bright. Her demeanor sparkling. Parts of her were pierced with pins and spikes. I imagined other places, not visible, but similarly pierced. Places covered in black and white and scarlet, fashion's rule. Her appearance communicated an assurance. She knew what she doing.

I forgot what I said when she asked again for my other plays. Whatever it was must have disturbed her since she blushed, looked sharply at the palms of her hands, then at the palms of my hands. A week later I received a check for seventy-five dollars and an embossed invitation to the reading of my play, which was to be fully staged after a few weeks of rewrites and workshopping (whatever that was). Someone named Jack, or Jake, Hall had been asked to direct. I was advised he might approach me with some questions. This prompted a little worry on my part since I had never actually attended a play in my whole life. Hundreds of movies of course, and the inevitable fifty thousand murders on TV. Accordingly, one day before I clocked in at the Reactor I drove down to the Wormwood Public Library and checked out the largest, and most serious-looking book I could discover on the subject of playwriting. It was called *Fundamentals of Dramatic Composition,* by Arthur Fit-Hugh Royale, Ph.D. A quick perusal of the this tome convinced me that the art was not beyond my grasp, and as both my GREs and SATs had been perfectly respectable, given my niche on the leading edge of Generation X, I sensed the way was clear. I possessed talent.

*

At work, however, things were not so happy. My nightwatchman's work was easy enough, but my jokes didn't go over so well at the reactor. The nuclear industry lacks a sense of humor. The business of the arrow; the ice-blue cool-aid; and the "hot" stuff in the water cooler. No sense of humor at all. Then the business of badges began. My first job at the front gate was pretty basic. Different color badge for each different level of security risk. I guess you could attribute my problem to a lack of discrimination in the color-blind department. I was supposed to make sure all white badges issued were carefully monitored, and usually this involved a lot of boring and pretty silly paper work. White badges were those handed out to visitors from the general public, the non-elect in security terms. It was a known fact that visitors from the general public could not be trusted to behave properly around a facility such as ours, as they were liable to breakage, mayhem and general run amok. They also were suspected of being agents from an alien power, an alien power with designs upon our designs, not to mention the approximately fifteen kilos of "hot stuff" on the premises. The hot stuff was plutonium, and it was stashed in steel buckets in the form of ceramic-coated, marble-sized pellets. Totally safe. Me and the other guys in Security often got pretty bored on those hazy, late autumn Sweet Thumb nights so we'd hoist a few, tell dirty jokes, and take out some of the "hot stuff" and fool around with it. We'd toss it around or roll it along the carpet in the canteen, like so many acorns. Plutonium is a powerful alpha-emitter, and feels warm to the touch, even through the thin ceramic layer. As long as you don't actually touch any of it, or breathe it in, it's as safe as handling any normal substance. Hell, we'd hoist a few and have a fine, old time. Frank, the Supervisor, didn't care much for the night shift, and would hit the Southern Comfort round eleven; by one he'd be sawing gourds in the land of nod....

Back to badges: red badges were ordinary staff (like me); green badges were management—the bigwigs and paper-pushers who administered the place, kept track of the books and signed the checks. Green badges also had the unenviable task of dealing with the frequent, noisy protestations of the white badges (those on the outside) who possessed even less of a sense of humor about the whole enterprise. Green badges were always trying to convince everyone, especially the white badges from the local newspaper, the *Tourniquet,* and the local CBS affiliate, WPOO, of our professional chops and the innocence of the whole operation; Plutonium's user-friendliness, and the facility's enormous economic boon to the whole, sad, impoverished, depopulated rustbelt region, et cetera (the woodsy summer camp-like atmosphere, et cetera).

Blue badges were for the serious, deeply knowledgeable few who actually knew what they doing, manned the control room and maintained order where neither white nor green badges, nor even yours truly, mister-red badged Christian Name, nor any other of the unblue-badged of mankind were allowed.

Around the time I met Puella Carpenter and began to work my gleaming vein of theater ore, I began unaccountably also to confuse the color of these badges. Whatever the origin of my sudden inability to properly discriminate it brought ignominy upon the name of Name at Sweet Thumb and opened for me a touchy can of worms. Particularly after I mistakenly admitted a delivery person from Fripp the Happy Pizza to one of the three Closed Monitoring Areas. Of course a blue badge sanctus sanctorum. Fortunately for me, the technicians who had ordered out had a sense of humor about the incident as they, too, had been hoisting a few. Still I doubt if inspectors from the Commission would have approved my accident.

By an odd coincidence it was the evening of the day after the Fripp incident that I attended my very first play at Gogol Rep. *A Burnt Angel Called Tempt Me* was the title; and it was written by someone from Arbor Vitae, Kentucky named Charles P. Charles who now resided in a Motel in New South Diameter, a steamy place near Cedar Key, Florida. Everyone in the play swerved and swore and sweated a lot; drank iced tea, wine in wine coolers and rye whiskey in jars. They tore open their greasy tee-shirts to reveal the remarkable wounds they had gotten in the War and show how much they loved the girl who was called "Tall Yaller," had been a nightclub singer before she lost all her teeth in a fight and her leg to a disease too terrible to name. All the men were called things like "Ganch" or "Banch" or "Danch" and they worked the old emotional marimba like a son of a gun. It was very impressive, like watching a gorilla knot a necktie, but not very life-like; it was also too long. Puella pointed out which performers had really shone, but being a novice I couldn't tell. In the dark the little, nice looking American-type small town set looked like a postcard. This is theater, I thought, terrific. Only I wish I'd known then, as I do now, that the trick with plays, especially the better class of plays, the realistic ones, is that they are supposed to be like other plays, not like life, which is insane. Mister Royale never mentioned this fact in his *Fundamentals,* which could have saved me considerable trouble, not to mention the trouble with my last, and most recent, staged reading.

The world itself is much too strange, much too strange for the world of theater.

Later on, we went back to her studio apartment in Palmyra and discussed the art of acting. This acting was all about "personal moments" and "sense memory" and something that was called "my through-line." One thing that Puella was very careful to impress upon me was that acting had nothing to do with make believe: Make believe was for kids.

I do believe that was the first night we kissed, on Puella's convertible sofa, in downtown Palmyra.

I was totally snowed.

And, the next day, the first day of my workshop, the cold reading was a success, or so it seemed to me. People smiled, slapped me on the back, and complimented me on my sensitivity, my deep and intuitive grasp of human nature. My natural ability to write from a strange and deep place.

Puella beamed at me like I was a new kitten.

I was in heaven.

True, Van Board, the Artistic Director, seemed disturbed when I mentioned, apropos of the protagonist, that what I'd wanted to accomplish, in his depiction, was to nail his ass to the wall because he was based on my bad uncle, Thornley.

True, the assistant director, Peyton, kept saying in my ear something about needing to feel more during the stoning scene. "These are real people, Chris, we have to feel more for them, in the gut department." True, the assistant dramaturg, Shively, whispered something I truly had difficulty understanding. "Where's the hug, Chris, where's the hug?" as he walked out into the blinding furnace of late afternoon, with a strange, gliding, snake-like gait, leaving me feeling guilty of some minor crime, like shoplifting or public indecency. Public indecency, a thing I would never do.

True, all the actors looked bored, utterly exhausted and hung-over. True, none of them spoke to me, except Carol who played the Fishhead and who corrected my spelling of "meropia". Still, I knew I had the benefit of some dark, occult force working for me, on my behalf, in the gut department. Now if I could figure out what to do about the hairs I had recently found growing on the palms of my hands.

3: [THE DUST OF ERROR.]

After another cold reading of my play (first called *Fishhead*, then something else), and a few weeks before the final, fully staged, reading, Puella informed me that she and Artistic Director, Van Rensalaer Board had a commission idea for me. Was I ever excited. It seems there was an intern from Eastern Europe in residence at the Rep; his name was Constantine and he hailed from the Republic of Perfidia, newly emancipated from the dusky embrace of the rotting Evil Empire, a land of fog, strong brew, and unusual, little wooden dogs painted in the bright, staring colors of the Byzantines. At least that is how I pictured the place when Puella first spoke with me. I had seen Constantine around the theater offices, but imagined him to be part of Maintenance, as he never said much, much I could understand, that is; and was always being sent out for coffee.

Chris, Van said, getting my name right for the first time; he used to call me "Greg". Puella and I have been thinking it might be good for you to tackle something different. An adaptation. Of a classic. From a foreign language.

But, I replied, I don't speak any foreign languages except the American, and that but flat-footedly, without grace.

That's the whole point of it, he grinned knowingly at me; sweet Puella grinned equally knowingly in the half-light, just over one of his padded shoulders. A talent like yours requires delicate nurture. He made a wide looping gesture with his hand, a big hard-looking hand, the hand of a man used to waving it around in other people's faces. A power hand. Puella made a similar gesture, but more freely. I had the impression they practiced these together to render them more authentic; and that, at least in this instance, it was Puella who had authored the gesture. Certainly she had authored the idea of the commission.

Chris, she said, We think too many young writers fail to develop because they do not attempt to stretch the limits of their craft. She made a really elegant stretching gesture, using in especial her fingertips. She looked very vulnerable and waxy at this moment. I cannot tell you how touched I was that someone should care so much for this thing called my talent. A thing that I with characteristic dislike of show would never have known I possessed. You would have to show me, and she did. It felt a little like being paid to go to the doctor. Only the gratitude I could feel welling up from the bottom of my shoes was so powerful I can hardly convey it. One result, however, of this sweet surrender to the lure of promise was that I didn't listen too closely to what was being said; certainly, in retrospect, not closely enough.

Van assured me that not only would my talent be stretched by taking on tasks such as this, tasks of adapting work from languages I did not understand, but also that my dramaturgical skill would be sharpened by hammering into dramatic form the epic legacy of the Cumans, the ancient Asiatic people who had inhabited the plains of Perfidia before their complete extermination on a single summer's day, early one midsummer's eve, in the fourteenth century. Constantine, who was not present at the time (the company van needed a tune-up so he had been dispatched to Whitlow, but that's another story), had done a compilation of the epic in his own tongue, High Perfidian. Money was available for him to transform this into a literal English version from the Rhododendron Foundation, a small publishing house in Tamar, the capital of Perfidia. A similar grant, for two hundred and fifty dollars, would be issued to me from the Mildred S. Random Foundation in conjunction with the Department of Turko-Tungusic languages at Groaner University in Whitlow. Puella showed me the manuscript, four thousand pages of single-spaced type-written text with extensive marginal notation in a hand I assumed to be Constantine's.

What we would like, Van was saying, is for you to boil this down to manageable size. Two acts. Approximately an hour and a half. No more than seven characters.

But, I protested, there are seven characters just named 'Uuc'. Puella shushed me with a compliment I did not grasp. (I had, by reflex, been leafing through what looked like an index while they were wooing me.) But's what's it called? I asked, as the title page had been forcefully torn off; and along the jagged edge there was a stain of what looked like blood.

Constantine did not actually prepare this version. He found it in the stacks at Groaner. Near as he can figure it has an abbreviated title, typical of the fast-paced, poetic style of the Cumans, *W's W;* but since the Cuman language possesses no "W", the contemporary editor and translator (whoever he was) called it *Q's Q,* as a close equivalent.

Do you know what it stands for? I ventured timidly, not wanting to get too far out on thin ice. There was a pause as my two benefactors exchanged glances.

Weird's Weird, said Puella carefully.

Who? What?

Weird's Weird, repeated Puella, with exact care.

Whose What? I replied and, Beg your pardon, fearing I had not heard what she had uttered correctly. Alas I had.

4: [FROM THE CUMAN TONGUE.]

Later, in the gloom of my little apartment in Whitlow, I allowed my fingers to lead my eyes as both crept through the strange, tattered manuscript with its strange, strange tale. Best as I could make out the narrative went something like this, squeezed like an idiot's fistful 'til it oozed forth:

Uuc, Son of Uuc, grew restless with life on the Great Drum Head where he and his people lived. One cool and windy night a terrifying meteor shower burst down through the Starry Mantle with the parable-message that he, Uuc, was a boring nobody and would never amount to anything, not even a mound of white chong pebbles, such as one finds high above the tree line on Mount Shadow Tiger (Tabun Bagdo, in Mongolia), a place sacred to their guardian spirits, the Bauls. Uuc considered this parable-message and despaired. He trudged off by himself into the Desert of the Hideous Flowering Greaseball, so called because in ages past, another man, a wiseman who was also a Wonder Chef, had had a crisis of illumination there while preparing a dish that employed the use of a hot, clay griddle. The Chef tripped in a lemming hole and catapulted his supper into the air whereupon the miraculous foliation occurred. The air-borne globule rose and rose until it soared high into the ether, where it exploded into a miraculous tuzzy-muzzy of Siberian gentian and pansies. This story occurred to Uuc also as he passed by, but it made him wrathful so that he stamped his foot and uttered the first of the nine-thousand curses that came to constitute the Cuman book of curses and cantrips, *Monkey Writing From the Time of Pyramids*. This curse was called Hammered Flame and was extremely useful against the left-handed enemies and agents of the unseen.

> Bingo, bingo, bem;
> Bango, bango, bem;
> Bim, bem, bum—

it began. All in all these curses took up quite a large portion the of manuscript and I would not be truthful if I did not admit to skimming some part of the material, particularly the endless, ornate refrains. Unwittingly, Uuc's first curse fell upon the father of his dear friend Tuku, a large and comical person who often posed in women's clothing and gave Uuc wise advice, particularly when the latter had worked himself up into one of his frequent, homicidal rages. Tuku's family arrived home from visiting political allies in nearby Pushtu, only to find their favorite child dead, neatly jerked inside out, like a leather glove. Uuc's curse had whizz-banged and scissored about in the transmundane region of Cuman Spacetime known as Qatqat; an eerie and drafty house of mirrors place populated by insane bats, malevolent, demonic creatures called Qats and various everyday items of Cuman crockery and odd hybrids of their household utensils, utensils come unexpectedly (and terrifyingly) to life. These were called Resonators and Phantom Sol-lickers, and they resembled ordinary forks and spoons, except they were likely to scoop a chunk out of you, or fling themselves with an awful do-ing! right through your forehead if you were not careful to curse them right back with the Cuman cantrip known as "Two Left Shoes." Uuc's curse got lost in Cuman Spacetime, whirled madly about in a neat 180 degree semicircle and pooped out from pretty much the same point it had entered; which was how it ended up aimed at Uuc's dear friend, Tuku. Nearest and dearest, in fact, of his left-handed camaradoes. Tuku's family was naturally not too pleased by this and called upon Odd-Man's Odor to revenge himself upon Uuc. Odd-Man's Odor is a minor divinity of the Cumans who generally lives in old horse blankets and Cuman underclothing, particularly after a long and harsh winter such as are frequent on the high, cold, windswept plateaus of Central Asia. Tuku's sister, Ta-Tuku-Ta, approached Uuc in a seductive fashion and while masking her cunning act as amorous foreplay, planted a certain bean, called a Heel Tapper, in his inner ear where he would not be likely to look if he suspected some-one of calling up the wrath of Odd-Man's Odor against him. Unknown to her, however, this par-ticular Heel-Tapper had been given long ago to Clq-Clq, the Girl-God of Sandals and Slippers by Moannumoannu, the Cuman God of Death in his "unmanifest" or Sleeping Thorn aspect.

Simply put, in this stage of Cuman cosmology, Death had not yet discovered his vocation and was a trifle confused regarding the true nature of his terrifying gift. Moannumoannu thought he was merely a local demon of the snowberry shrub and fawn lilies. The bean which he had given to his paramour Clq-Clq had been tossed away by her, since she found him a clownish oaf and did her best to spurn his advances with taunts and mockery. The bean rolled off into a meadow in the Shadow Tiger Mountains where it lay hidden for a long, long time. Ta-Tuku-Ta must have found the bean accidentally during one of her frequent sojourns among the steep green defiles of that region; or it may have been given to her by one of her paramours among the pastoralists of the region, called Speckled Hypachilians, since it was an established fact that her erotic tendency found its ease among these gloomy but colorful mountaineers with the habit of wearing a swath of tattered silk as a sash, and of painting the left side of the face scarlet, so that when they faced North to give their praises to the Bauls (who were thought to live there) they might also greet the setting sun, Lord Anafract, with a special and comely and cosmetic declaration. Whatever the origin of the bean Ta-Tuku-Ta planted in Uuc's ear, it proved a fateful bean; for it was the Bean of Morpho-Liquidation, and so could be returned to its rightful owner, with the unstated and priceless promise, from Moannumoannu, to redeem all the Chosen. Those who grasped its power. Unwittingly, Uuc stood on the very brink of immortality and could have saved not only himself, but all humanity had he simply followed the set of instructions, the Inwit of the Baul's Bean, that were displayed clearly on the monitor of his consciousness at the moment of implantation, or soon thereafter, at the moment he recovered full use of his faculties. Alas, as was his custom, Uuc became enraged at the images dancing in his head and began the wholesale slaughter of all those nearby, whether Cuman, Pecheneg or Avar, so that by the time he succumbed to the narcotic effects of the bean and grew tranquil, the terror he had created was all out of measure and no one wanted anything to do with him, or his apparently crazed ravings about the power to undo death which he contained in his head.

So when Needle-Holder, of the Tribe of Cray-fish, lumbered up behind the Holy Maniac, as Uuc was now known, and beheaded him with a stroke of the Blade of Pure Negation, no one had the wit to comment on these ravings as Uuc gathered up his head, still muttering madly, and set off for the Ice Mountains to heal himself. The secret of this special Heel-Tapper was forever lost on Uuc, who entrusted the precious bean to an Umbrella Bird named Wolf Wing after he had roundly cursed Clq-Clq with the curse known as Bruised Lips, thereby incurring the wrath of Moannumoannu. For the god suddenly awakened to his power and flung a truck-sized pluton of hot magma at our hero. It missed him but levelled the golden city of Nenuphar, city of sweet clover and narcotic flamingo scat ... and on and on, in vast paraphrastic loops. No wonder I grew dizzy and had to lie down, a washrag shrouding my bumpy face.

What am I to do with this?

Q's Q, a play impossible to write.

At this point the haze of delirium begins to press in upon me—so that I feel like Uuc, who had unleashed Death by a foolish misadventure with immortality. Foolish, brutal, stupid Uuc. Of the rest, during these recent weeks, I have little or no memory. Except at the discussion following the staged reading of my *Fishhead* play, when a nasty fellow in a red fez (one of my actors?) said my characters were mere bouncing puppets, devoid of soul; and another young fellow with upside-down glasses asked, was my play a real one, or had I made it up?

I remember Puella laughing nervously at that. I meant to reply, that in truth it was a real play, but of the tribe of Uuc. I am told I made as if to bite, bite the young man in question.

As for the late artistic director, I do not think I am responsible for his death. I do not think I have the strength, human or superhuman, to do what is alleged to have been done. To him. Poor Doctor Board, may the angel that slumbers in the snowberry and fawn lilies sing for him. But if am further hunted I can promise you this: I have seven sticks of dynamite girded about me, and my glittering Smith & Wesson. I am a man as good as my word. Name is my name. What I am saying is no idle threat. No mere show. If I go, so goes the Number Two Reactor; and if that goes, so does the whole valley of Sweet Thumb, and all that's downwind for a hundred miles. We who fall into the category of the perennially promising are mean suckers once we're cornered. I hope someone understands the situation

Q's Q, a play impossible to write. Weird. This is truly weird. Weird beyond weird.

II: Perfidia

5: [THE DUST OF WHITLOW.]

Behind every hero, said Lord Voljac, is a snake laughing in the grass. It is now three years since I first saw an American in real life, Doctor Board. He was on a visit to my country, Perfidia, known for its paprikas, politic-complexity and for the puppet theater of Tamar where I grew up, a grower of cabbages. I did, however, not stay so long with family in the hamlet of Gorod, near Plizent, no. From an early age I am observed by the authorities who notice my talent for the mimetic arts, archery and free-hand large-bore rifle shooting.

At the International Festival in Blin I am a representative of my country. There are Germans, Russians, French, English—who know everything about how to make theater (according to ancient rules of Shakespeare and J.B. Priestly), some Africans and Jews—I don't like them; and Doctor Board, who is a fine soft-spoken American with a big handshake and eyes like a *chukchuk,* the fierce wild turkey of my homeland.

Since I am tired of my long training period in Tamar, and have no friends or family in the local political apparatus, I know my advance in the art has impact a wall. This is truth. Go to America, says my Aunt Vera. They have money there, and only a thin layer of top soil between them and the veneer underneath. You can teach them a little of our ways, many of them come from here, from places like here, but they have lost the anchor of the land. And the smell of our cheeses. One cannot be a true Perfidian without knowing how to butcher a fat hog while dancing the "Ta-Tuku-Ta." These dark things of the earth connect us to our sad stories, the murder of Lord Voljac and his shadow cabinet, and the tragedy of the recent World Cup when those black Africans from Brazil dynamite their own stadium rather than allow Perfidia to vanquish. Score is 3 to 1 with eight minutes remaining. If Lord Voljac had been there they would not have dared to do such a thing.

Doctor Van Board has seen me in a performance of Bulgakov, as the cat. Then in a version of your own American play, called *Paint Your Wig On* presented in a barbaric chewing gum factory, just inside the border from Russia—or Ukraine (same damn crowd: old, old enemies of us—the People of the Scarlet Handshake)—downwind of the Chernobyl Reactor. Great Director Soldan, a disciple of Vassiliev, has rehearsed us some two years. This is a nearly perfect perfection of a production, after the stage manager is shot as a provocateur. We don't talk about these things generally to Westerners. You have no understanding of the problem of the vertical and horizontals, and how the life-force in the etheric-membrane is like inhabiting the mask of Uuc (from the Cuman days—we killed them all).

~

Van Board is my friend, a man with artistic vision and unlike most Americans, a person of discrimination. He can appreciate deep thinking, as that of my cousin, the old philosopher Cermak, a friend of Beckett, Cioran and the madman, Witkiewicz. Cermak's book is called *The Dust of Tamar*, an exegesis and cross-examination of various meaningless molecular entities drifting this way and that in the Perfidian air, in the form of a Socratic dialogue. In truth, Beckett, Cioran, and even loony Witkacy have stolen all their ideas from Cermak, particularly the work of his young and passionate years, *On Blight:* a shrinky-dink of the human soul considered as a fruit left out too long on the window-sill. This great genius is misunderstood because he opened the gates of Tamar to the Nazis' 10th Armored Division Commander Von Bulow, with the ancient glagolitic curse: "Death, make all a desolation behind me." Miserable muslim swine in Parliament interpret this as an act of treason, when it is clear he was making an ironic comment on the lost treatise of the Avars, *Nnuptil's Kneecap*—a witch's handbook describing methods of torture and mutilation commonly employed against their powerful foes, the Byzantines—a subtle slap at the Nazis' "Drang nach Osten." These Muslims condemn him to silence after the war, and make him dwell in dark sub-cellar of a private lunatic asylum run by, yes, an American—Doctor Thornley Wolfe of Molossus University, inventor of the Universal Counter-Septic Lozenge known as

Pepto-Bungo. Resistance leaders of Perfidia have attributed our stout obstinacy against the Nazis to mildly addictive powers of Pepto-Bungo lozenges, or U.C.S.L.'s. A troublesome side-effect of this lozenge is: scrotum turning bright green, teeth become enlarged as a tusk or fang, and much loss of sleep because of nightmare of history flooding uncensored and unstoppable through all intellectual orifices of the human consciousness in question.

Cermak meet with Heidegger in the Black Forest during the Fifties to correct some mistakes in the concept of *Dasein:* Cermak is convinced the clearing of the unconcealed must be hidden again under huge, war-surplus camouflage net— to protect it from the nosing around of certain unclean peoples, peoples we would not want to name because it might get us in trouble from naive General Walker T. Mallowcakes, a Unitarian minister too simple-minded to perceive the "miasmus," Uncle Cermak's term, of undialectical history.

Humanity is disgusting offal, my good cousin informs Heidegger, who replies, only a god can save us. A god with horns, says Cermak and these two geniuses toast the same idea, clink glasses of a rare tokay Cermak has kept hidden with him, as receptacle of some small hope, amidst laundry baskets in that sub-cellar in Tamar.

I think Van Board understands the depth and wisdom of Cermak. He have an option on an early work (and the philosopher's only dramatic work) called *Hammered Roadkill,* but his Board of Director's—those people are so typical American in the wishy-washy style of their compromises. They do not like the scene where the young Muslim children are fried like ginks in gingily oil, like butter fish, can you imagine? It is due to cousin Cermak that I have studied the history of the Cumans, heroic pagans unaffected by either Byzantine decadence or Mohammedan false gods.

Americans need the moral complexity of your Uncle Cermak, Van Board tells me, and I believe he is right. Not to mention the hero of our brief independence, Lord Voljac. You cannot eat a cat until you first have flayed it, he warned us. I and my brothers have taken that saying to heart. I carry an ancient Glagolitic glaive with me, even to America, as I suspect to follow the wisdom of my Uncle Cermak, the dust of Witlow is no more clean than the dust of Tamar.

6: [THE ERROR OF SELECTION.]

Van Board, this wise big-handed man with the
droopy yellow moustaches, shall have take me to
America, where we shall exchange ideas and,
hopefully (though I am too modest to say this), I
shall become like him, a rich man capable of
wearing soft shoes Italian leather and Scotch
tweeds. This droopy man is my friend, and I confess I have read between the lines of his modest
and incomprehensible way of talking; as in "I
never met a man I didn't like" and "Give me lib-
erty and give me death" and "It ain't over 'til it's
over" and "The theater is no place for diverting
spectacle; it is a place for painful speculation" and
"Just know your lines and don't bump into the
furniture"—all these statements are a mystery to
me until I actually become a resident of the United States and learn how to behave, more or less,
as one of you.

But I confess Whitlow and Palmyra and other
places, even the great metropolis of Chenango
seems a poor place to me when I arrive here.

Suddenly I understand the great sadness of Americans who inhabit this dreary and joyless prairie. It is such a poor prop of a civilization against the fury of the icy wind that blows down from the North Pole, through the desert of Canada, to here and further.

And what tiny, poor theaters, and how badly made. I cannot believe the poverty of them and the cheapness of construction. It is a temporary world, of portable toilets and temporary sinks and temporary smiles. Like Dilly; she is a good kid, though she has no taste in dramatic literature. I like her smile, with its teeth. But she does not understand what a theater is for, and for that I do feel pity. This play called *A Burnt Angel Called Tempt Me!* Everyone in it is named "Ganch" or "Danch" or "Ranch" and they wear the ripped tee-shirt of their miserable childhood in Oak City where the evil father make them drink their own pee-pee and snivel against the Lord Jesus under the balloon of night, during the cackling lightning storm. Then the daughter fall in love with the visiting Man From "Moon-Bake," Montana who weeps three times—all with great falseness—because he cannot sell the objects in his suitcase, these Unconical Vee-Eight Girdle-tailed Gin Blocks, from Whipple County, in New Delaware; and this despite their superiority to the competitor's model, the All-American Pie Constant-Motion Boston Gin Block manufactured by evil snake-oil baron Jake "High Stakes" La Delray from Smokey Keys, Ontario. And there is the pathetic and hollow scene where Anna Carolina overcomes her polio, walks to the front porch and either 1) gives "Yanch" or "Branch" a promise of the blowjob while kneeling in some corny moonlight talking about How Great These United States Are Once Mister Edison has invented the lightbulb, or 2) render ecstatic prayer to Old Walkingstick, spirit of Volopuk Indians from which she is partly descended owing to a passionate errand into the wilderness on the part of her great-grandmother, the actress, Nora Grindly, of saloon notoriety in nearby Wolf-Maw (now Palmyra). This is a perfectly terrible play, but has won the Wurlitzer Prize and the Megalith Award from the Guild of Contemporary Dramaturgy—whatever that is can you imagine?

I have seen plays here we could not imagine in Perfidia. Plays so thin you can slide them under the screen door when it is locked shut. It doesn't seem to matter to these people. Everything they do seems to please them, so I conclude the Americans are a people too easily pleased. The absolute worst is such a drama of confection as this *Fishhead* play by the young Chris, this very stupid young man who Dilly has been talking to me about regarding *Q's Q*. This person is **analphabetic** as regards the art of Dramatic Literature. Such a sweet human being only, like others of his kind, there is no sense of destiny, of a here which is not a now. A sense of belonging to a place that cannot be cancelled by a failure to... to be happy. This passion to be HAPPY, among people like Chris and Dilly, I find it hopeless. It makes me feel sad.

But then who am I? My homeland has been destroyed so many times I am dizzy at the thought. Here I am, dwelling in a silly square, ugly box-type structure near the Palmyra Motel and the Palmyra House of Eats, surrounded by four walls which are cardboard; square in the middle of a forest of hairy trees I don't know the names of; speaking this language that hangs on me like a suit too big, and of a pallor like the skin of grapefruits; even my most universal torments cannot find satisfactory expression here because I have no special facility in this tongue. And all day people are treating me like an idiot-person, like "Constantine, can you fix the water-leak in the Ladies' Room?" and "Constantine, can you take these wooden boards in a pile near to the prop shop for Mister Calvado, the Technical Director?" and "Constantine, can you go next door to the Diner and get coffees for Mister Van Board and Dilly and Mister So-and-So of the State Artists' Council and Miss Who-the-Spoon who is from the Board of Directors?" and so forth and so on. None of them are aware that I am the leading genius dramatist of my generation in Perfidia. And since none of them have any interest in anything not directly to do with their American idea of how to get rich and be happy they will never ask me that one question that will allow the true truth to pop up can you believe it?

Sometimes at night, I go out in the cornfield that is across the highway. Sometimes then I walk there and take off my mukluk shoes. These shoes look like small, battered tool sheds in the silvery moonlight. I walk among the cornstalks talking to myself in my own language, and am not so lonely only a little. I feel like the moon is a wandering Moon Man like me, and has tried to keep me company. The moon of this time of year we call *Tsinna Moopa,* the bowl of curdled mallow thrown against a wall, the Black Wall of Mister Death-Stick, the bogey who built the staircase of magic squares; the top box of the cosmic weasel-trap whose poisonous spit keeps off those wicked creatures, the Vvilliki, who snap at us and scrape at our steamed-up windows in mid-winter from the place where they have been tethered forever, in the Outer Dark. Things without the certainty of shape, and thus forbidden by God from real being. So: I see myself, darting about, reciting from my poetical works and the ancient curses and litanies of my people, half lost in the shadow and moonglow, like some strange bird with my odd and unAmerican face, face like a pair of pliers when viewed in profile, and my wild Perfidian hair! My wild Perfidian hair that is always standing straight up like a brush, or runaway bipedalist broom. My hair that can never be parted or combed. Hair that no amount of American fashion-cream can make to lie down and behave like normal hairs, like the hair of ordinary people one sees in the drugstore wearing the clip-on bow-tie and searching out the nailclipper with which to use and so avoid the habit of biting on nails, a thing that all Americans do without full consciousness, like the picking of the nose in public places. None of us in Perfidia would do such a thing. It is a thing for which we reserve use of the hanky, polite.

Yes, when I have some perspective on these matters, I can make a little sense of it. Sometimes when I think of the Americans, and of the moon-faced look they have on their round, expectant faces, I think of the big balloon festival which is held near the mall, just off the highway near the Sweet Thumb Nuclear Reactor at the far end of the valley. You see, all those fine, intelligent, somewhat rich people assemble here from Lord knows where. Boontown, Denver and New Delbert. Big and colorful balloons, all the colors of the spectrum, with friendly sun-faces, in stripes or speckled like they were flags of some foreign country of people who happen to live in the sky. Each balloon has a basket lowered beneath on heavy wires, ballasted with sandbags, and propelled by a vertical gas-flame jet that cause the entire apparatus to rise. Some few of these airships are modelled on animals, dogs and cows and fishes, for example. I have seen them also in the form of a giant tennis shoe, of the kind worn by the giant Negro-type person who is so famous he makes all the money there is in basketball. Others are in the images of stars, cubes and the *Ursus Theodorus* which is so beloved of American children, but which reminds me of winter in the crag region of the Gliin Mountains, the province of Paaarv, where one of my cousins, the poor illiterate woodsman Tronka suffered a great wound in his hand while fighting a vast, brute, brown bear for a few scraps of dog meat after an avalanche had trapped him there, alone for three months with his quite few wits and those big, ambitious bears.

So: I am amazed to see the sky over Sweet

Thumb and west, towards Whitlow and Palmyra and over the enormous, flat black malignancy of the parking-lot at the Great Wind Repertory Theater, a building which belongs to no known family of architectural principle I can tell you about; further, further and further still to the smoky outskirts of Chenango itself, of which your acclaimed poet C. Q. Mallard wrote: "O Chenango, Boiler of lake-water and the steam-boat's huzzah! Crusher of idle feet and careless dreams like the sledgehammer's Ho, Ho, Hop-Hing!" All the purplish, cloud-stuffed skies are filled with the slowly floating hulks of these empty, dreaming apparitions. Apparitions of apparatus—silent except for the occasional *foosh!* of their blue-tipped gasjets; all eyes raised to watch them, majestic; bland and tubby like the balloons themselves. All these round, happy moon-faces gazing, gazing up at balloons full of hot, hot air. Hot air and nothing else. To me it is like a metaphor for some basic spiritual disability I could not affix a label to. Because if I could it would sound wrong coming from someone such as me, only a humble guest and therefore obliged to be grateful even though there is much here that is meaningless or that I despise. I hold my thoughts, carefully, like pickled turnips in a leather portofolio next to my heart. I pat down the wilderness of my wild, ungovernable Perfidian hair, and try not to think too much about Dilly's slender, white ankle; her white calves and knees.... I discipline myself with the consoling thought that were it not for my passion and genius for the theater I might just now be laying naked, shot in the brains, or hanging from a tall fir tree, on a hook, having been flayed alive by all those ruthless Muslims at St Displicip's.... "Water washes blood," says Cermak, "but both trickle down the hillside and into declivities of slate and... malachite; water and blood trickle into the deep, still pool of truth at the center of the world. And no one knows what these trickles of water and blood have to say, and no one has any idea what to do about it—except hack down the Mohammedans, hack them down to the last, poor, wailing, gesticulating beggar among them."

7: [MAKACHKALA.]

As intern at the Great Wind Repertory Theater, I
am learning how to make my way in this world of
non-thinking liberals. Soft-type thinking people.
I have learned that the essence of democracy is
that one must speak my mind not too much, otherwise people get the idea you want to get a leg
up. In especial, I have found that no one here is
interested in the deep things of the heart, Cermak's philosophy for instance. They look at me
like I am deranged when I recite the aphorism:
"There is no make-believe in Makachkala" or
"Flaming horses leave a trail of smoking cinders"
or "No man knows what the demons do under
his nose-hairs." Freedom makes people careless
about deep things like the anniversary of your
own death, dead swans and especially what they
mean, mold upon fresh dimpled things, unprece-
dented eclipses, hexylrecorcinals (used to purge
worms), accidental death by hiccups, blight—and
the wonders of blight and all her works.

No, no one here speaks what they know, about dark truths.

Except me. I am the only one.

Listen to what I say in regard to things. As for instance, I know something is the matter with this madman-situation about the Theater and I know this long before the Evil Deed has been committed. I do not know exactly how it is going to happen, but I can feel it coming. The people who attend this reading series of bad plays, organized by Dilly—as I call her, not her ridiculous school-girl name of Puella Carpenter—are all very strange. Bitter. In the talk-back sessions they speak in tongues, and concerning what? It is uncertain. As an example I will lay the backdrop. First play in the series is called *Scaly Legs* by Bornius Fragholster, a published poet and Vietnam veteran, partially confined because of monster eating disorder contracted on tour in Southeast Asia. This play is about one "Skeezo," formerly perfectly average-type American guy (School of Ganch) who barricades himself in Mens Room at the Capitol, strapped in dynamite corset to protest his transformation by evil political shenanigan. Vile, corrupt, bigfat Senators must come and hear the life story of this citizen and learn. His humble beginnings (especially spontaneous gang-rape of town-slut, Foxy Handlefire, a lyric moment before he loses innocence in South-east Asia), et cetera. Americans like to lose their innocence over and over, but where they find it in the first place no one can tell me. No man can say, no man can say. Chris had admired this play very much.

Big Actor from Chenango, John Dough, is the President of the United States and suffers a partial loss of hearing as a result of this gut-wrenching drama. Chorus of Viet-Cong ghost claims they are proud to be torched alive by such a man. He apologizes to former fianceé; she has been beaten up 'til somewhat brain-damaged, and they are married, to sound of church bells, in Beaver Valley. This girl, Jerky Jane, is made State Bird of the Commonwealth of New Baskets by Governor E. Potable Jaywalkingstar. He announces: Never will a drop of our dear boys be spilt fighting for the Yellow or Dark races on their far distant, illegible shores. Now, audience members like this drama and are astonished by its graphic application of rude violence. It seems the habit of beating people silly about the head part raises the thought of similar infraction in every one present. All confess to bad thoughts about paper boy, girl scouts selling salacious cookies and so forth and so on. A gentleman with strange hat offers the opinion that all this is the work of the Devil. He means the representation not the activities represented. Others agree and offer to burn the place down using a common incendiary device manufactured at nearby Varmint Torus Variolite Rendering Factory (P. J. Booph and Sons). Whoa, whoa, says Dilly as the playwright is sweating hard through neoprene longjohns. It is the function of art to diddle this doodle (or some such), she says. The director, Nevius Hogflatter-er, is a big man from Chenango, and offers to program the entire **ouevre** of Mister Fragholster, it is so riddled with untainted and inexcusable passion. Dilly also speaks a lot about passion too until the grumblers are silenced, look low about the room, muttering among themselves as Americans do in the presence of someone who they feel to be superior, despite their hard wish for this person to die can you believe it?

A man in a dayglo ski parka jump up and down, saying things all about this is stolen from his own masterpiece, *The Pohai Vapor Lock,* which he outlines in some detail for the unenlightened; it seems *The Ten Commandments, Pulp Fiction,* and Cloghutter's smash hit of Great Wind's last season, *A Box Within A Box Within A Box* are all thinly disguised misappropriations of this man's seminal work. Many people, especially the ones with floral head gear, make a succession of linked, slightly overlapped, gasping sounds at this, which saddens me because I am trying to make my way through the crowd in order to greet Mister Bornius Fragholster in order to suggest he study the history of Uuc (as presented in my modest abridgement). The arrival of riot police and up-ending of several tables of Great Wind's promotional materials discouraged me in my attempt at split-the-gap. Or, later: the reading of *A Moo Unique,* the family chronicle by one Iris Ible Icefield, an elderly person with enormous, wise hams filled, as she has kept repeating, with the true stuffing of life. *Moo* features many fine woman actors, also not too many of the "Ganch" and "Branch" variety, which is a pleasure for me since I cannot understand their low accent like the long, low and curving drivingway. Anyhow, all these ladies are hat makers in a big city called Wallbash. They fall in love with men who make shrubs for a living (this is true) and make love with them in the Handsome Harry (deer grass) and haricots—this is very elegantly told till we learn they all have succumbded to a dread disease, Fusible Exopathic Pemphigus, a tragedy. So: they are all dead even as we do speak. This causes much emotion in the audience, and human sympathy for the victims of Time's Furry. I do think though, at five and one-half hours, it is more long than it should be. Others would disagree, as did Dilly, my friend. But in a certain portion of this play, there is one good scene (and one interesting character), the scene of the wild, slightly-stooping madman, called Dexter Sinister who makes a prophecy no one can understand, nobody but the dumb (unspeakable) sister, Wen Penny who is otherwise a useless person; she becomes, so to speak, covered with hairs as a result.

Wen Penny says: A murder will be done upon the person of a Big Cheese. This seems to me a foreshadowing of the actual drama ("true life," you say) of this month, which was enacted by Chris Name before he fled. I cannot read the soul of man, said Lord Voljac on his parapet at Luiigu, but I can break him on the wheel. A suggestion I was too shy to make after the reading when Mister Van Board express doubts concerning the central core of the play and its comprehensibility for those of the audience unfamiliar with Iris Ible Icefield's complex iconography. Indeed, the saying "There is no make-believe in Makachkala" has to do much with the Autarch Haiduk's habit of painstakingly dismembering those hapless balladeers who disremembered the meaning of their ballads and fol-de-rol when summoned to do so by him, "Hawk Frown," Voljac's Uncle Haiduk. He was a man suspicious of things more complex than they ought to be. It is like the old song from the people who worship Lord Fear in the mountains.

8: [THE WITCH WHO WALKS ON WOODEN LEGS.]

But I am not conveying correctly my impression of this heinous murder of my good friend, Doctor Van Board, the only man who truly cares for me, the lowly Perfidian Exile and Intern, in this cardboard jungle of American. Life is difficult here despite what it says on the television only no one seems to know it. All the saw mills in Palmyra are being boarded up, the Yo-yo factory will move away to South of the border and I can tell by looking at the farmer's field that the topsoil is giving out, all washed away. The only places that are actually growing are the landfills near the Interstate, and in the shadow of the slagheap. These are such big humps you cannot imagine. Big ones like animals who have sunk into the earth because maybe of their titanic weight, creatures from the old days before the flood—antediluvian beasts like the antique Megalodon they have mounted so strangely in the rotunda of Groaner University. With great crinkled face and iron plates soldered to the side of his bulk like rows of slate shingles on the mosque at St. Princicip before we blew it up. Americans are like this great beast and the secret kinship they feel with such creatures is a thing I have been thinking about. Back in the Sanjak we are not interested in such things—the church has opined all these bones are from the Devil Time, and modern philosophy prefers to let old bones rest in the dream of Oblivion uncommented on. It is the human past which consumes us. Ask my Uncle Cermak: The reading of shapes in the dark stone leads to the madness known as Tripping Over the Devil's Jump Rope—a bad thing resulting in instances of head-Butting, mouth full of foam, and insane case of declaiming romanzas concerning several horny vegetables (squash, pumpkins and one very much like the New Delbert calabash, a mighty fruit).

Yet, each of my friends here, each and everyone (and all unknown to the other, as if it were a low, common thing like the public nuisance of public urination, or vulgar burping, or drunken howling) have acted strange and secret concerning this interest in old, antiquated saurians. Dilly, Chris, Mister Van Board and even Lydia Yaddo Darkwood, from the Board of Directors, all have taken me to see their proud personal treasure, the hunchback Megalodon at the gloomy rotunda of Groaner University. Generally the conversation goes something like this:

The smiling American turns to me, all teeth glittering in the gloom like the Megalodon:

Well, Constantine, isn't that just about the most big doodle you ever have daddled in your whole life?

Well, Chris (Dilly, Van, etc.) it is QUITE a remarkable instance of the monster...

Betcha, you don't have creatures like that (indicating the Megalodon with the initial digit—a habit, I confess I find very nervous making since back in the Sanjak it is not a thing one does; in fact, if you point your digit at the wrong person (Lord Voljac *par example*) it is liable to be the last thing you do. A frequent cause of the famous Perfidian blood-feud is to be discovered in the wanton wagging of the digit, wanton and promiscuous waving of the digit is deemed an outrage beyond apology among our hill people; so I always feel a palpitation of ancient dread in the vicinity of the flagrant initial digit)—back in the Sanjak.

No, Dilly (or whoever), Back in the Sanjak we do not dig up those things, fearing the curse of the witches who put them there to spite us. Maybe it is different here. You Americans are a toothy people and so the existential connection may be a thing of wonder for you. As the piece of the true cross is for the Christian peoples.

But, Constantine, those huge reptiles once lived here (there goes that digit again—this time pointed to the center of the earth—a bad, bad place according to the stories of our forefathers). Right here, right here, says the excited person as though a single place separated by two times were any more special than two places connected by one—like the Sanjak and Bezuckistan (home of our ancient foes, the Pziinipls). Human fate is a nightmare, whatever.

This is a thought of which I do not get the point, and so I explain why using a brief slice of Perfidian history: the conversion, miracles, trial,

mortification, drawing and quartering and cruxi-
fication of St. Pereplut now worshipped in the
Holy Mass of our Perfidian Church despite her
archaic origin as local cheese goddess of the Gol-
di people.

You see, Dilly (or Fred or so on) for us, there
is no membrane between us and our past. The
Dead are standing quietly among us, in the crys-
talline robes of the Upper Air, hissing and crack-
ling. Their loves and passionate hatreds go on,
and on. They whisper in our ears what it is we
must do (and like a fool I spoke all this to poor
maniac Chris who is not so good in the head!);
and if we do not do what we must they mutter
among themselves and move our feet, one by
one—as if we are marionnetten—and raise and
lower the forearm and elbow whether we wish
them to or not. This is the way things are; this invisible band will clutch your hand with the dag-
ger clasped in a fist they have gripped tight, hard,
around yours; and when you hamstring the foe,
and then silence their cries by slashing the throat
vein, there is a perfect pretemporal synthesis of
Person in the now with another frozen, seeming-

ly, in a history we cannot fathom, nor gather up in our wit's hands, like fiddleheads. It is like the battle of the baseball... and the bat, to illustrate by reference to your National Sport, even though some of its principles seem a bit foreign to me. Rooted in a corn myth not current in Europe.

But, she says, what is wonderful about the animal is that it lived far, far before us. At a time so remote we cannot even imagine it.

Dilly, I say, I cannot imagine a time so remote I cannot imagine it and furthermore...(this always makes the American, each and every one, break out into a rapturous and wild speech about Time without boundaries; but we have stone gods, Terminus and Hermia Thermex who stand and block the end of all roads in the Sanjak, and such metaphysical dithering; you must kill a cow or cock to go further).

Connie, Connie (That is what Dilly has called me.), gee...doesn't it seem like a marvelous *possibility* that worlds exist within worlds we never dreamed of...it's like in Shakespeare and...the *possibility* that as we think we diddle we are only a-doodle and that long, long, long, long, long after we are gone and all traces of us, too…so on and something. A cobweb of vain hopes.

But usually by this point I have gone blank and so they go blank too; because the Americans are a polite people with too many teeth—and besides such a train of thinking is not capable of extension much beyond this of diddle by doodle without its great derrick tipping over and crashing to the earth so the metal spikes of its big shoes are pointing up to the stars.

I think this a highly commendable monster I say, and pat the beast gingerly upon the hindparts of it; pat it gingerly because in truth, because in truth the face scares me too much. Perhaps because it suggests something about the human face I would prefer to let rest; perhaps because it reminds me of…of Baba Jaga: she is the reptile hag who lives deep in the forest. When she wants to go someplace she poke her feet, which are claws like those of the Megalodon, poke them right through the floor boards and pick up the hut, and go waddling off making a very strange and scary sight to see, with vine and broken branch swathed around her, with bird's nest and full of moss, lichens, dead leaves which have gotten stuck to it. The hut is made of leaves and human body parts which have been sawed off (and up); and cured so that they look like lumber. On top of the house (near the chimney which is a tower of meshed rib-cages and vertebrae) are the skulls. And when I see a skull I know that skull is trying to tell me that there is a thing I must do. And mostly that, if Baba Jaga—the one who eats up people who get lost in the woods—is the one we are discussing, is not such a good thing.

I like your bones better with the rest of pretty you hanging on them, I say to Dilly; and reach for her hand. But now I recall when Chris Name bring me here and I finish the exegesis of Baba-Jaga; he suddenly looks sad, like a man who has had a dream that contained a message. I would not like to be an American selected by such a dream as Baba-Jaga instigates. How can you obey the Demon who commands you when you cannot understand the language she speaks and she refuses to use yours?

My friend Chris's name, Name, is of the type we call Fallal: nothing good will come of him except the art of being a very nice man. He has taken me to see baseball games, to play miniature golf, and drink the green beer of St Patrick's Day; and to discuss race-relations in America—a thing all Americans like to do despite the fact none of them actually enjoy having dinner with the person of a different race. My views on this subject I try to control, but it is hard. Without a sense of history Americans can simply not understand our determination to stand firm against the Muslim. They have never heard of Kossovo, and the names of Alp Arslan, Murad or Mehmet the Conqueror sound to their ears no doubt very quaint and very far away. Not to us. You cannot explain it. Lord Voljac, during his brief reign as Emperor of the Sanjak of Perfidia, gave us back our sense of race-pride. We are the tribe of the Eagle, he said, and our nest must be the impregnable faldstool of our falbala and falciform afflatus.

My friend Chris understands the words (some of them) I speak, but not what they say. I don't blame him. It is a truth that is hard, and it is a long shadow that creeps along behind me and my people. Fear makes us no wiser than you who are transparent with your wishes like the candles on the windowsill on the Eve of St. Agnes (Anya, X, Dragii), poor delusion.

This shadow is the shade of the Sanjak.

I tell Chris, Just because you don't see the silhouette forming in the frost on the windowglass, or out there, behind the elm tree, or underneath your parked Saab and, indeed, behind your eyelids, does not mean it is not so. All this is an intellectual mechanism. All this rinky-dink of dovetail-joint, all this dowel, sprig and dowel-pin is an ephemerality not worth a tinker's damn bought with one thin dime.

In any case, I am the first and most lowest on the apparent rung of the apparent stepladder at the Great Wind Repertory Theater to ascertain that there is a dangerous personality at work here, apropos of Mister Christian W. Name. Am I a genius to perceive this fact? No, merely an astute person of modest perspicacity who is not blinded by reading my own promotional materials. To whit: Chris's habit of talking such obsessed incoherent blah-blah about his job of work at the Sweet Thumb Nuclear Reactor, a very peaceful and well-managed operation if you ask me; clearly all this talk of "possible melt-downs," "leakages," and "unauthorized emissions" has more to do with the instability within his own brainpan than of a few, harmless radionuclides hopping about, nearby, in the earth's atmosphere. Next there is this young gentleman's obsession with all aspects pertaining to lycanthropy, were-wolfishness, and other Children of the Night so called. We in the Sanjak have a deeper perspective on such matters believe you me. We know false *ordog* from real one, and do not talk slightly of *vlkoslak* and *vrolok* when we mean something else: possibly insane garbage collector and other practical jokes. The odd way he talks, for instance, as if hair were growing on his body parts; on the palms of his hands, it is true, but I am not impressed and suspect, as I have reported to him, it is merely an outcome of not correctly washing his hands at the Reactor and will go away with time, like the Bulgarian Itch. But the third of these fixations is most strange and not to be found in any of the literature on dementia (I have visited the Medical Library of Molossus

University and can read well the language of these scientific texts) known to me: it is a quality I would name the metastasizing of the descriptive appellation, in the title of the play department. All these famous intelligent dramaturgs do not even notice: I do.

First his play is called *Fish,* simple enough; a little dry and perhaps a little fuzzy in the information department. As the chief dramaturg, Clarence Withwhistle, is used to saying, "What are we to make of 'Fish'," Chris? Does it jerk at the heart-strings? Does it remind us of when we were small, weak and covered over in diaper rash? Or does it suggest our current lives as large and competent things, bobbing in the brook of life's continuum of commitments?" And so after the first cold reading *Fish* became *Fish-head* the second (a lukewarm one) it was now *Threw the Fish-loaf;* "Head" became "Loaf" because the dramaturgs thought the idea of food made the play more homely, hence accessible. The "threw" made it more active, hence daring. Always a plus in the American theater where the notion of risk is at best vestigial. Then after a consultation with

the second and third dramaturgs, Morton Bie-
dermyer and Fitz-hugh Lammergeier of the prestigious Mandible Players in swank Lenore, New
Delbert (Famous, of course, for its *Dewdrop Fol-
lies*) it became *Threw the Fishloaf in the Fire*—an
act of defiance now clearly indicated (even
though there was none whatsoever to be discovered in the murky, semi-pornographic heavy-met-
al chronicle of Thaddeus IV, Emperor of Mars).
A consultation among all three dramaturgs resulted in a change of "Loaf" back to "Head"—
someone in marketing had made an innuendo
about serving Palmyra's growing Asian-American
community and so Clarence Withwhistle (fearing
the whole thing was getting a little too fey) suggested an addition, postpositionally in grammati-
cal terms, of Generation X lippiness and attitude:
Threw the Fish-head in the Fire because; Dilly ad-
monished that given the colossal stature and
delusional grandiosity of the Emperor's great an-
tagonist, Mister Adam Atlas Hillsman, an adnate
might be advisable, an "I" anterior to the rest,
apparently to avoid a left-leaning domino-se-
quence of toppling abstraction, hence: I *Threw*

the Fish-head in the Fire because. But I could tell, indeed, who could not? that there was something totally aberrant, something dramatically unsyntactical with his brain, when Chris showed up for the final rehearsal of his staged reading with the title changed once more: *I Threw the Fish-head in the Fire because It was Looking at Me Wrong*. This sounded, to me, like one of the curses mentioned in *"Monkey-Writing from the Time of Pyramids,"* or something from the medieval astrological treatise by Astragalus that Cermak used to consult before going abroad, when he would take the baths at Baden-Baden.

To sum up: his metastable title-habits (exacerbated, to be sure, by dramaturgical meddling) indicates a progressive sublunar imbecility masked as a mere episode of logogriphy, known as Caroline's Disease. So, when the booing, hissing, tittered laughter and carefully worded admonishments that the piece "needs work" faded into stillness; I was not surprised to see a new Chris—a Chris I have never seen before!—lurch and falter to his feet, mumbling what I instinctively recognized as an ancient Turko-Tungusic language (it did occur to me it might be the demotic Cuman of my own *Q's Q*), and lash out in a dark, hoarse voice to ask for the Prehistoric Megalith of Moannumoannu. And also, for him, the dark Vizier of the Dead, to discharge that Precious Bean, the mighty "Heel Tapper" known only as the Bean of Morpho-Liquidation with the hirsute thong of his divine sling, so that ALL become a desolation before him.

It was then that the small theater riot began. The coffee machine go crack, slipslapslop on the floor and guess whose job it is to clean up? Chris has gone. Piff! And Dilly is talking to Doctor Van Board whose big hands are looping crazy-eights, and the actors are complaining to the Stage Manager (only "hip" person—in the cool-jazz sense of "cool"—in the whole place) who is fiddling with her silver nose-ring and trying not to listen; and the three dramaturgs are intensely conversing in their private language—and this language is a Special Fruit not to be found on any branch, twig or rhizome (offshoot) of the Indo-European Tree; no, it is a cultural anomaly. Like the Sloop-Rigged Univariate Unipod Argot of the Shiny-

Leaf People, who collect soapberries on the slope of Mount Mardu-Sundik (also known as "Shipman" from days of the Great Game).

The rest you can read about in the Police Blotter of the Whitlow *Trapezium,* a greasy publication. Like Cermak says, History works by gravity feed. For myself I cast no blame, leaving that to the demons of the Vvilikki and Qats, both of whom will tear the evil-doer limb from limb once they find out who he is. All I know is Lord Voljac would be proud of this new man hewn from the wood of walnuts; this new Chris, a man.

III: Dough$_2$

9 [AN ACTOR PREPARES TO PREPARE]:

Artistically Speaking, I enjoy being stretched, you see. The actor's art is neither appreciated nor understood in our time. Especially in these miserable provinces. But, in any case, all the really juicy roles go to New Yorkers. At Groaner I studied Sense Memory and Affective Memory with Glory and Hugh "Ray" Mann. Stankus was before my time and he was, in any case, rumored to be quite gaga well before his retirement, poor duffer. Then a year in Britain at Barking Dogsberry and the Royal Institute at Basingstoke, where I studied Merovingian Movement with Modred Kelleher. In the meantime he's been knighted, but alas we're no longer in touch. I am the only actor in the region—New Delaware, New Delbert or New Dumbo—with a certificate in Merovingian Movement. And, for the most part, training programs in the tri-state area are a joke. Mainly stand-up and silly stuff. Young women wiggling their fannies, and the school of Higher Holeration. Not the deep, deep stuff of the immortals of

Glory's generation. Strasberg, Donderbeg and Professor Bach whose masterpiece *Mister Depravity* premiered at Groaner while I was there. A deep, deep play about deep, deep things; Chekhovian in the mellowness of its mallow, its sad truthfulness. For Professor Bach always demanded truth, the whole simple truth, even when what was at stake seemed, to the untutored, to be a bit more complicated. His adaptation of the fool scenes from *King Lear,* for instance, where he rewrote the Bard so that a real conflict could emerge, and the sad tale of Festus' brutal childhood among a family of violent and demented tinkers could be told, at long last. His exposé of the abusive behavior endemic to the jester trade in those days simply broke open for me what the art of theatre could be. And so at Groaner when I played Holdsclaw in his masterpiece *Mister Depravity* I felt I had come near touching the stars. Little did I know what lay ahead.

While at Groaner I took the stage name John Dough, for Dough pronounced "Duff" is an ancient and honorable name among us Middlewesterners, us Hickeys. And obviously I could not call myself "Hickey," and the first name is even worse. We will dispense with discussion of the first name altogether, although I am sure it will pop out at some point, as that is the way of the world.

Anyhow when I graduated and began to audition for parts on plays I made a shocking discovery: there was another actor by my name, and so accordingly, by the rules of the craft, the name belonged to him, because, because, because it must be so. By order of linear priority, an aristocratic axiom. So Equity, our union, has decreed. As a half-measure (until the demise, at long last, of my namesake) I have adopted the superscript, or is it the subscript? I am officially John Dough$_2$, and so am listed, officially in the Equity books at their offices in Chenango. My original is a company member of long standing at the Rep there. On principle I refuse to see his work (for fear of an unwelcome influence, although on occasion I review his reviews, mostly favorable I must confess). Obviously this is a situation I find problematic, but there is nothing I can do about it. Once, however, Mefius Crinkle of the *Press-Ponentior* did offer some rather snide remarks concerning the "wavering insecurity" of his Devonian accent; the play was Thornapple's *Bohemian Rose,* adapted by...by another Thorn, or Thornley, some black Irishman of the hour.

I do know where he lives, in the Arcadia Apartments on North Shore near the Elevated, a mixed neighborhood currently in economic free-fall owing to an overleap by the new Interstate (Route 99, the Stockyard's Corn-Chute). I have examined the dumpster behind his building and scrutinized his utility receipts. His phone number I cherish, though I have never ventured to call. I am haunted by the idea of his voice—his evident skill at playing Shakespeare (Iago, Brutus, Malvolio), Brecht (Azdak) and Leadhaven (Monsoor and the Dork of Cork). As to his sexual preference there is ambiguity, a fact suggestive of the chronic, convicted switch-hitter; he drinks single-malt scotch, but not excessively, and red wine. He does not drive, or if he does he does so under an alias. Could it be "John Dough" is not his name either? I am told he pronounces it "Doe," and is a charming, if under-sized fellow, in a wedgy, unremarkable way. Not quite a star in Chenango's heaven, but certainly not a cipher either. People, friends in common, say we should meet, but no, no. After so long, it would be of no use. And I am convinced the downward turn of my career, despite my expertise at bicycle, improv, rings, Spanish web, vocal ventilation and Merovingian movement, has something, something indeed obscure to do with him.

He is older than I am, by six years; and so I reckon I have ample time to prepare. Preparation is everything, Ray used to say to us, his disciples at Groaner. The once in a lifetime part must not be rushed, even if it elude one for the better part of that life, that life of preparation. A life spent as a waiter at the Century Club in Palmyra; the occasional voice-over for the ABC affiliate and whatnot (I am the voice of "CHOOZ" a kind of chewable local cheese byproduct, and the local symphony); the occasional musical at Summergarten, the local community music-carnival, and readings, readings, readings.

~

I am quite sure, on the other hand, that my insidious other, John Dough[1], does not prepare for the parts he must play with my diligence, silence and cunning. For he must only enact the roles; I must prepare to enact the actor himself. In order to assume the mantle of my true name, my stage name and not that other, that Hickey—Frog Hickey—there, it is out.

Names, name.

Nomination, all of it so problematic and so, well, farouche. Or do I mean Louche? Bother it. But the conjunction of the previous thought, readings, with the current one, names, brings to mind the unfortunate circumstance to which, I suppose, I ought to address my Thespian meander. Is that well-Englished? I suppose not; they know better how to order these things in London, well. All I know is that through the murderous connivance of a Name, I have lost my one true employer, Van Board. Affable, waxen Van, the only man in the whole tri-state area with whom I could discuss *Coriolanus,* or *The*

Changling, or *Perlmutter's Spawn of Priam, A Trojan Prophylactic.* For it was in the name of that ignorant knave Chris that all this came about. I will not point the finger, though all the world knows who it is that did the deed, and why. I was at that fatal reading, the terrible reading whose grisly precipitate was poor Van's dismemberment and death. His mangled *exeunt* (is that the right tense?).

The dizzy dramaturg is the cause of it all, with her obvious crush on that rube, Chris. Who would imagine a mere staged reading could occasion a riot? Who? Who? Who, who watches over all this non-for-profit nonsense; and I assure you it was not that mediocrity Jake Hall, from Wolverhampton, who directed the silly thing, and struts his stuff at all the garden parties in Mercator Heights, and at the luxury condos of Bromley, Beaver and West Palmyra. When did Jake Hall, grr, that pretentious and mannered Avant Garde bore, grr, ever cast me in a show? While the likes of Mellor, Moonly and Jane Jesus Hemphill routinely haunt the boards of the Rep, the Roundabout and the Annex ravishing the classics of every conceivable kind with antitheatrical gargle and Parkinsonian Amble? The only Dough known to Jack is Dough[1]—case rested.

Van alone truly respected my difficult craft, and now poor Van is dead.

10 [WE GO DEEPER INTO MY STUFF]:

Okay. Okay. I never actually attended the famous Groaner School of Drama, only matriculated (is that the right word?) at a summer school session in Radiance and Rhetoric: a Seance on Elocution, but Glory did give the initial lecture. He really did. And I did study with Roy—Hugh Mann. I really did. In fact, after I left Groaner and moved to Chenango, I joined the famous Workshop. No one cares much about Mann anymore, grr, because the more famous gang in New York, Strasberg and the Actor's Studio crowd simply stole our fire (or is it wind?); but Hugh Mann was the first to truly crack the nut of the Method, the first to reveal the pithiness in all its pulp. We met for a month in a vast loft down on Century Boulevard, near a truckers dive called "The Shark"; it quickly became our hangout, and we had good times there, man to man stuff, mostly. We chased out the skirts if they got too vocal. Roy was clear about the ground rules and about the preparation, and if you were a skirt you knew your place. Matter of fact, we guys inaugurated the kind of guy-acting Chenango's still known for, the earnest, torn-tee shirt acting you see in all these knockoffs of our improvs, Bugs Murphy and Stu "Killer" Steinbach's plays, both Wurlitzer winners. But we didn't need plays to make great theatre, and mostly the plays we rehearsed were junk anyway. That was fine with us; you could never figure out what they were about anyway, and you broke out in a sweat just trying to read them. You get honest with me, and I get honest with you. And I'll tell you straight: no one really likes Shakespeare because, grr, you can't understand it. It's just all this talk. You hear me, talk. All those Greek plays. Not a single true moment in all of it. That's what we learned at Roy's workshop. After we got evicted from the loft we rehearsed for a summer in a abandoned airplane hangar past Jerusalem Grove out near Route Three. That was great, only I didn't have a car, and often had to thumb a ride. My day job was typist at the Associated Press, and I could keep my own hours pretty much so it worked out fine. Those were great times for me. They knew me as

"Jules" Hickman and I felt accepted for who I was, and the deep stuff inside.

Incredible, Roy would say after a scene, I've never seen such truth. And I could feel the glow of truth radiate from my pores. My favorite scenes were the fighter pilot's death-bed scene with a young nurse whom he first thinks is his mom, then his sister, then his grandma, then his dog "Bounder"; or the learning impaired boy who, being last in line at a gang-rape, was the only one to get caught; or the son who has to explain to mom why he always felt different from the other kids—because dad was a communist and probably also a fag. Because the truth I could muster for these improvs was such deep stuff, I was an underground celebrity. Other Method teachers and actors would drive hundreds of miles to see my work. We'd hang out, get drunk, have fist-fights and carry on. We'd chase their skirts, and they'd chase our skirts. We never could find a play that was right for us. All the big plays in those days were talky and, well, faggy. Or kind of jerky, or kind of jerky and dumb. Williams and Albee and that other guy.

We were evicted again, and things got rough. For a month or two we met in an abandoned meat locker, which was confining but very visceral. There was something very appropriate about getting into our deep stuff in an abandoned meat locker. But the group started to fall apart after that. It's funny how it happens, you find yourself with a group and everyone's real tight and you confront them about their hang-ups and they confront you about your hang-ups and you break down barriers and learn to open up and all this deep, deep stuff comes out and, hey, you turn your back and everyone's gone, split, vanished. Bill and Studs and Cal and Hank Simmons, a real good actor, Hank Simmons. He gave it all up and went to refrigerator school. Now he's got a mortgage, a family of four and a fast track on the rat track, poor chump.

Every now and then I go back to that meat locker; it's still there, out behind the Walmart at the intersection of Cushman and Beryl Heights, near the Zoo and the Masonic Temple. Looks like a piece of detritus from the late war, or the tomb of some Asiatic notable. No one ever called me Frog Hickey there.

~

But for me at least Van's murder rhymes with another, that of poor Roy—Hugh Mann. This happened some years later, late sixties or early seventies. The Workshop was much smaller now, and we never showed our work to anyone. But that was fine with me, concept directing and **auteur** directing and political plays were all the rage. Babe and Rabe and *My Heart is a Wooden Leg* by Noble Ricketts, that ass. I had come out of the closet and flirted for a few years with Higher Gaiety.

My stage name was Lorelei Hickey, and I was the Azalea Girl at Nicky Tardive's very swank nightclub, "Obelisk." I also enacted various personages in the late-nite revues and sketches that were so popular. Lady Ottoline Morel, as the Queen of the Fairy Circle, and so on. That lasted for awhile, and the sad question of my training receded for a time. Glory never entered my mind, not to mention Stankus. I got a postcard every now and then from Roy, inviting me to return to the group. Somehow all that seemed a remote and not especially cheerful episode in my life, not a place I wished to return to. Funny, how the twists a life takes when there's no apparent torsion left in the old apparatus. Then Peter got sick, and I moved out. Sick people, I've never been able to endure them. And I've always been healthy, despite whatever style of life's currently my practice. And the ongoing nature of my preparation seemingly prepared me for them all. I pass no moral judgment on the ill, for it is nature that has done that. And you really cannot *explain* to a person why you find him loathsome, anymore than you can to a person you no longer love. But gay life was coming to be seen by many as not so gay, so I sought counselling through the good offices of Ron, at Aesthetic Realism. Aesthetic Realism and Ron taught me that I could be cured of my costly perversion. And so I was. The whole thing was easier than quitting smoking, though I do confess to stealing the occasional cigarette. On the sly, of course, And I never buy cigarettes, but only borrow. And I only borrow from friends, never strangers. And rarely that unless I have had a glass of wine or two.

~

Having come to my senses, I realized I would never come to anything without my Group. The dull sting of my three-time rejection from the Groaner School of Drama—there! It popped out! Damn, that's another one of my nasty little secrets. The dull sting of my rejections has predisposed me I suppose, to such associations. Affiliation in groups, group-type activities. Theatres are basically like groups, except the groupers involved come in several distinct species, according to their standing in the establishment. Actors, unless famous like Chenango's own Hartley Dunes, occupy a rather low rung in the whole.

I like a place where no one calls me Frog Hickey.

But for me at least, Van's murder rhymes with another, namely that of my mentor and friend, Hugh Mann. My Roy.

11 [THE RAY OF ROY: A RESURRECTION]:

One day, at a Group meeting, Hugh Mann stood up in the middle of Mitch Goff's improv, said Jdark, and died. Too bad because Mitch was cooking, everyone swore. What his improv was concerned deep, deep stuff about how Mitch had been beaten by his Aunt Nectar with a coathanger for not eating his vanilla junket. You know it's deep stuff when you know it's *vanilla* junket. That specific. Me, I was having an interior smoke, and just plain missed the moment until I heard Roy crack the glass on the coffee table (by now we were holding our meetings at Roy's condo on Wilshire in Rome, with its twelve rooms and stunning view of Lake Wachovia). Cracked the glass in two, ditto for the satinwood frame, and just lay there, just lay there. We figured he was dead by the way he didn't breathe or move. After I returned from the toilet—my delicate nature and problematic relation to illness necessitated a loss of lunch—we sat around discussing what to do. And there was poor Mitch there, sobbing his heart out. He had spilled his guts for Roy, but would never get a critique. It just didn't seem fair. So we sat and talked, and slowly figured out what to do.

~

Within a few hours our tight little group had ratcheted down (or is it up?) several notches, and we had become what might be described by an unsympathetic observer, as a cult. Only we had no project to pursue in the big world, no sublime or sacred message, no millenarian or apocalyptic agenda. Whether the world prospered or foundered was all the same to us. No, our sole mission was the Revivification of Roy, so that through the Ray of Roy (a difficult concept to get across to the uninitiated) we might resume our training, our training for the only task that seemed worthy of all the deep, deep stuff we had collectively gotten ourselves down into; name the task of ongoing, and perhaps life-long prepara-tion. Using pipe cleaners, cue tips and hairpins we fabricated little tiaras which we then sprayed with gold paint, one for each of the seven remaining disciples of Roy. We were transformed by this tragedy, into Seven Tongues of the Ray of Roy, his filamentary flamelets, star-tipped flashpoints of pure spiritual preparation.

Within a few days we had constructed a massive bier that occupied most of Roy's diningroom and adjacent livingroom. This we assembled from things we found, mostly by the side of the road. And it is amazing what you find by the side of the road in places like Rome, Palmyra or West Nutley: thousand-pound slabs of cement, discarded home furnishings, including toilets, sinks, bath tubs, tables and chairs of mock mahogany, a New Delbert Dual Forklift Suspension chassis, and a whole lot more. We dressed Roy in his best, black worsted suit and propped him up there, on the bier. Every few days we replenished seven vases of flowers (much of these expenses we managed thanks to Roy's handy Bank of Rome ATM card; his code, SYOR, was not particularly difficult to figure out).

We chanted and sang; we chanted and clapped and sang; we chanted and clapped and moaned and sang; we chanted and clapped and moaned and yodelled and sang; we chanted and clapped and moaned and yodelled and whistled and sang; we chanted and clapped and moaned and yodelled and whistled and did the herky-jerk and sang. We modelled and yang. For days and days, we did these things and lit candles and made burnt offerings and burnt sticks of sweet incense and consulted the stars and observed the movement of the wind in dead grasses the color of a mouse and read the steaming entrails of small semi-domesticated animals we had lured into the Temple of the Ray of Roy, at his condo on Wilshire in Rome. Seven weeks passed, and nothing happened. Nothing happened but that Roy kind've shrunk up and wilted, like a piece of ripe fruit left out too long. A fruit gone pulpy.

~

One day as we sat around trying to decide what to do, long after the point of discussing the whole thing had come to seem, well, pointless, we had an illumination. And there was poor

Mitch there sobbing his heart out once again. He had spilled his guts for Roy, and now he spilled his guts once more. And yet again, he would never get his critique. None of us would ever get our critiques, and yet we knew we must go on, and on. We must go deeper and deeper down into our stuff because there was no way of telling how much of it there was, nor how deep you had to go to get to the bottom of it, or across the vast extent of it, or bore through its bulk to pop out on the other side. I think we all learned a little bit about courage and determination on that day. That's what I told Mitch, and Mitch said something similar to me. Pretty soon we all had come out of our state of being stuck. We realized that the Bad Place is the state of being stuck, and that doubt is a bad thing you do with your head.

~

Several weeks later a police officer appeared at the door. It turned out there had been a complaint from neighbors in the complex. There was a difficult moment or two because of the candles, and our tiaras, and the bier and flowers and other things. Not to mention Roy there, not looking too good.

12 [THE TRAGEDY OF MY TRAINING, CONSIDERED AS THE FAILURE OF WHAT WAS TO REAPPEAR]:

No indictment is necessary, fortunately in a case like ours, namely the Making of a Public Nuisance (a simple misdemeanor in this state); although I am still convinced of our innocence as the nature of the nuisance was definitely private, even venturing on the clandestine. It was difficult under the circumstances to work up much enthusiasm for a spirited defense as most of us were broke, exhausted and spiritually blank by this time. For me the worst part of the whole proceeding was the necessity to hear, over and over, in the presence of my fellow disciples, the appalling vocables of my odious given name—Frog Hickey. For after the humiliation of this revelation I knew I should never be able to face any of them again. A lot of the trust you build up with people you are in the habit of getting into deep, deep stuff with depends on little moments of truth-telling and the trading of factual information, like one's real name and how one came to be, thus, denominated. I had told them a whole lot about my family origins, us Duffs, and how we emigrated from Cheddar in Somerset; and before that, some equally noble and ancient municipality in Eastern Europe, once part of the former Evil Empire, the town of Quilq (also, by coincidence, a kind of cheese) in Western Perfidia—the part settled by East Goths and Cumans from Central Asia. I had borrowed some of this information from an odd fellow, Thornton or Thornsomething, I had met while doing summer stock on a tour through the drab and wind-bleached agricultural wastelands of New Baskets, and the even more drab and sun-bleached cattle and mining towns of New Dumbo. Places with names like Scissors, Hair Hat, Golf, Potato Row, Dark Man's Gulch, Leadville and Snake Hill. Creepy, low places where you'd do a medley of scenes from Shakespeare and contemporary lesser classics, from Merritt Person's *Popcorn My Poppycock,* Glock's sappy romanza, *Harriet the Beanpole.* This guy had done some adaptations for us, based on A WINTER'S TALE and a bunch of scary Perfidian ghost stories. We were tempted to cut a lot of the scarier scenes, scenes with carnivorous eyeballs on stick legs, rivers of blood and murderous flying forks. But in the end the kids loved this kind of thing. Kids always do; kids and cats love to be scared, even if the material is ridiculous and third rate.

~

Exposed as a convicted memory fabulist, I knew I would be dropped from the group. Wishing to avoid this I fled and spent some months working as an Entertainment Coordinator aboard a cruise ship, the *Demeter*, which visited a dozen or so glamorous ports of call in the Caribbean and the Gulf of Mexico. I recovered my strength, morale and suntan giving group lessons in Merovingian Movement and Spanish Web to crowds of nearly indistinguishable retirees from places like Toronto and Moonhat. I directed scenes from the classics of all cultures around the shuffleboard courts and the full Olympic-sized pool. Odd rumors of a strange man on board, a strange man like none of the others among passengers and crew prompted my creative juices, and I began to make notes for a play or short story I would write. My long years of preparation had convinced me of the fact that there was very little in the corpus of American dramatic literature worthy of the name, and therefore I had nothing to lose.

My literary effort concerned odd bits and pieces of standard Americana, combined with some delicious bits of Perfidiana. A certain unholy bean which when planted in the ear of the unsuspecting causes double-vision, hebephrenia and an insatiable desire to the practice of theatrical mania; the tale of a very good man who goes to sleep for a very long time and when he awakes discovers to his great surprise that he now is evil, or that of a very bad man who goes to sleep for a very long time and when he awakes discovers to his great surprise that he now is virtuous; or that of a very sleepy man who succumbing to drowsiness slumbers undisturbed for a very long time, centuries perhaps, and when he awakes discovers to his great surprise that he is still asleep, or awakes as a wedge of cheddar cheese, or as a pitcher of blood; the tale of the animated set of mechanical teeth, teeth which set off on stick legs cross the hills in search of something to bite; the sad tale of a common North American amphibian with a wine-splash birthmark who hippety-hops all the way across North America to study with a certain Prince of Vocal Arabesque and Ventilation, and Proper Devonian Elocution; the tale of a cheese with two stick feet who walks all the way to Rome to speak with the Pope (Boniface XII in my version) concerning the Higher Things; the tale of a poor actor from Baghdad who seeks out a wise old acting teacher who inhabits a meat-locker in order to go deep, deep into his (the acting teacher's) stuff only to discover that he is a mere two-dimensional drawing, a drawing made of dots connected by lines and squiggles, lines and squiggles characterized by a wavering insecurity; the tale of a strange man, either bat or wolf, who tears his kindly old boss limb from limb when the latter (incidentally the Artistic Director of the very same Repertory Theatre in Chenango where John Dough[1] haunts the boards (isn't that fortuitous?!)) saws the air with empty gestures and fills the night with hackneyed vocables, vocables from the Pretty Times Done Did. But I did not get far with my serio-dramatic fol-de-rol; for as my outlines began to take on the quicksilver quality of an epic...an epic in the aspic of endless *repetitio,* one glorious flan-colored morning off Cedar Key a fax arrived from the Rep here in Palmyra, Great Wind Rep, requesting my presence for a series of staged readings of Contemporary Classics, aspiring quasi-classics and other New American Plays (NAPs). The author of this invitation was none other than Van Rensalaer Board, a classmate from those happy days at Groaner (have I got this right?) where I first felt the urge to unbare my soul before whomsoever, and get deep down, deep down into the lunatic's peat-bog that is the human heart. And so I once more revised and updated my CV, and set off for this part of the country from that, as open to exigenous (is that a word?) fate as my training would permit. The idea of starting my own group occurred to me also, I must say. I knew my duties at the Rep would be demanding, but my new power and prestige might enable me to jump-start my second career, like those of Glory and Swanhope, and the renowned Hugh Mann. Who knew? Who could tell?

~

Once in residence at the Rep, and barely unpacked and unboxed, I began to see my situation in a totally new perspective; that the tragedy of poor Hugh Mann consisted in more than a mere failure to reappear, but in something far, far deeper. I began to see that our failure, and here I am talking about both our initial group and its later crystallization and reconfiguration under the aegis of the Ray of Roy, was that we were unable to find a *modus* whereby to share our deep, deep stuff and our commitment to the ideal of Permanent Preparation with the community at large. Van's genius was to see that one did not need, after all, to produce plays, or not many at the Rep (and these from among familiar chestnuts), but that an appropriately conceived staged reading of a new play must provide the most efficient vehicle for the unlimited, open-ended preparation we seasoned actors knew most likely to keep alive the ideal of preparation for its own sake. No memorization (a problem for **moi** in any case since I (like my doppelganger) had developed a taste for single-malt scotches) and the all-too common tyranny of the director of today, usually an arrogant dolt unfamiliar with the noble traditions of the acting profession, and often a slavish idolater of the "text," as some arid system of signposts, sign posts determining performance. Determining performance anachronistically, nay hegemonically. A notion so out of place in the better-class of theatre, as to be risible (risible, is that a word?).

Accordingly, and by virtue of my immense experience, rendered plausibly enough on the pages of my vast and elaborately adumbrated CV, my presence at the Rep began to be more and more a controlling one; a controlling one in all areas of play selection, development, talent management during the touchy rehearsal process, and during the inevitable devastating critique that would follow. These young and frequently lower-middle class semi-literates were simply no match for me, and my colleagues in the company. And yet we were able to share our stuff within the community, a community that applauded our generosity even as it disapproved of the typical NAP as formless, ill-conceived and all in all a botch and more of a cultural symptom than a work of art. My colleagues (and I shan't bother with the names because most of them are provincial types, poorly trained, bygones of hope gone bad and perhaps an ill-placed promise of promise—losers, in the main) found ourselves in the wholly enviable position of being regarded as, well, experts in all matters of taste, style, emotional truth, intellectual appropriateness and, well, even writing itself. A subject I now came to realize has been my true object all along, as unbeknownst to me as that character in Racine who discovers late in the course of it that he has been speaking "prose." Only the occasional meddling dramaturge, and I am referring to that Carpenter bitch, a bitch on wheels, and visiting nabobs like Jake Hall, grr, that pretentious autocrat…that visible embarrassment to all things Thespian, only intrusions like these disturbed our little frogpond at Great Wind. And this was all Van's doing, even if it were mostly my doing on Van's behalf. Because Van was generally too preoccupied with bureaucratic stuff and the necessary but onerous task of fund-raising to bother with artistic policy and other details. And so it would go: Shakespeare and Chekhov, both perfectly respectable vehicles, and not too chestnutty; then the occasional NAP, Grouper and Elbowe were my favorites. The former wrote for GASSY LAUGH, a truly funny comedy show in the 60s; and the other, a Wurlitzer winner for a dreary, though touching play about a trip to Lourdes, which manages to touch touchingly upon no less than thirty-eight distinct kinds of disease, abuse, retardation, and other, obscurer, forms of abjection—all them touching; even if the play,as a whole, rang false. *Night-train to Lourdes,* it was called, appropriately enough, since the journey involved a night-train to the holy place in the title, and featured as narrator a demented alcoholic ex-street person hopelessly addicted to the classic street-person's beverage also announced in the title, "Night Train," not, of course, "Lourdes" which sounds more like a brand of mineral water.

~

But then "Pooh" enters the picture, disturbing both me and my circles (who was it that said only the angels walk in true circles? Saint Jerome? Saint Viar? Saint Stanley of New Delaware?) with this ghastly Fish Head play, absolutely the worst piece of drivel I have ever written (I meant to write, read), worse than Williams or Spider Robinson. And I am supposed to play Thaddeus, the Lear-knock-off presiding over a crumbling empire, on a planet ruined eons ago by nuclear weapons. Can you imagine the idiocy of that? Lear itself is bad enough, with its illogical and cruel gaffs of bad taste (and what, pray tell, are we to make of the Fool with his lunatic natterings?); but this appalling clunker simply defied all...all that pertains to training itself, preparation and the getting into of deep, deep stuff. What affective truth can one come up with, grr, for a

Martian character? Nay, what Sense Memory? Van and I quarrelled over the matter, I will admit. I felt betrayed, and compromised. Hell, I felt he cut my dick off, and I guess I told him because he said he felt like I'd cut his dick off too. We left it there, I guess, both of us feeling wounded and like guys walking around with their dicks cut off.

As for the murder: I never would have been capable of an act like that, even with my blackouts and periods of insane rage (the source of my own deep stuff, Roy reasoned) and superhuman strength at these moments, no. But then I must confess I still cut a fine finger (is that a malapropism?) for a man of my age: hard belly, wavy chestnut hair, teeth—a lot of them real.

And I've got all I want, like the High Priest in Claggart's *Niobe,* with his fine speeches on Mutabilitie, and how all things change to remain the same, a wheel or something. Or something like that. Joshua Claggart, came a little later than the Bard, and writes a whole lot clearer if you ask me. But I never would have been capable of an act like that. Even if he was asking for it, the swine.

Still get sick, you see, at the sight of someone...someone ill. Speaking of ill, I saw Peter on my last visit to Chenango, for an audition (did I get the part? No, grr). We talked a little, he's on the street now; he doesn't look so good.

IV: Pooh

13 [DILLY, AS IN DALLY]:

Funny how people call me names. Connie calls me "Dilly"; Van mocks Connie by calling me "Dally"; Chris calls me "Pooh," presumably by reference to my Christian Name, Puella, which in turn was the bright idea of my mother Grace, a Latin teacher at Groaner Prep Day School. Dad, a Greek teacher, did not object. I have grown used to Puella, and since no one in the tri-state area knows what it means, I am relatively safe. Girl Carpenter: I should have that printed on my business card. Girl hammerer of nails and boards! Dramaturgs rarely have need of a card, for though we counsel wisely we are not ones to push. We must be discrete, and leave the glamour and razzmatazz to others. It is the oddity of our dramaturgical lot.

In the attic of our large, tumble-down farm-house at Palmyra, I have discovered boxes of old snapshots. Of my parents and grandparents, and me: sunlight-blinded, flaxen-haired me with my straight line of a mouth, hands full of expiring violets and dandelions. My parents and grandparents all wear reflective aviator sunglasses and gawk, awkwardly available to the rapacious lens. Even then I distrusted such intrusions as a kind of violation, even as I ravaged the flower-beds and their wilder cousins in the shadow of the cottonwoods; I was a true felon of flower-pickery then, perhaps as a compensation?

But for T. T. Blackthorn's system, lord knows what simpleminded and girlish (but entirely false, false, false) mask of easy grace I might now be wearing. My whole family, even my sister Clarel and Dred the dog are a mystery to me, a fearful enigma. Since the successful application of the good Doctor's P. T. Hypnosophic-Hypnosis and the recovery of my submerged self, I am reluctant to lay blame; but blame there is, and it must be acknowledged, in order for proper therapeutic closure. And true, they all hate me for what they did to me, all of them, even darling Dred, that salacious scottie. Entirely unaware of the dithering moil and batweave within. My personal trauma has been eased by my political idealism, and in particular my ardent devotion to the figure of

Christy Todd Whitman, who I do fervently believe will triumph as the first female President. But then I don't like to talk about my political beliefs around theatre people because theatre people are all so Politically Correct. All so mediocre when it comes to the discussion of important social and political matters. All so self-obsessed and poorly read. And mostly, so untalented. And talent is what it all comes down to, isn't it?

So, part of the healing process I have re-visioned for myself includes talent, and its discovery and the translation of it through the magic of craft (craft is one of my lodestones) into art; and more formally, the legacy of art: art history. Early on, at the water-color and finger-painting stage and despite my parents' continual (and problematic, one might say) proddings, I came to recognize my own profound lack of talent. Artistic barrenness, I came to regard it, naively; although given the way I now perceive the situation, it seems far more complex. Most people, however, have the most appalling blinders, and are capable of the most appallingly ill-considered judgments and misconceptions and prideful lurchings to and from the altar of high art. Frequently it is a trauma similar to mine that stands leering behind, leering behind in the shadows, breathing heavily. This knowledge of the dark side of our human condition makes one prickle up and pucker. Anyway, in my own small and relatively unimportant way, I do believe I have and shall continue to make the world a better place; it is not my boldness and arrogance that has announced this truth, but my talent-like obsession with craft, and all things crafty, and all that pertains to form. I say "talent-like" to make clean and clear the distinction between what I do and do not possess: talent, that miracle-gro of the true imagination, that great strong grasp of the truly seizing imagination. The wolfish imagination, one might call it, all shaggy and fierce. Imagination in excess of ordinary imagining and the general level of hit-miss imaging.

And so I am obsessed, in my discussions with the promising young playwrights I meet, with things like the "spine" of the play, and how to nurture the playwright's Sleep of Reason and Inner Dream. Things I studied at the prestigious Groaner School of Drama under the great men there. Earle M. Glory. Herbert Swanhope. And especially Joseph Leadhaven, the genius Leadhaven. The spine of the dream of the play, and the dream of the spine, not to mention its sleep of reason. These topics came to fascinate me; and above all, what the ancients termed *Catastasis*. Catastasis and Pre-catastasis (my specialty, and the subject of my dissertation later on, after the scandal, at Molossus University) and Post Catastasis, the theory of Wuvorin, author of *The Cheese of Baghdad*. This wonderful vocabulary writ on scrolls of gold and mother-of-pearl adorned my heavens, along with the plays of Brecht and Shaw, but especially the works of Glory and Swanhope; both masters of all varieties of Catastasis. Would it be out of place for me to suggest a further application? for who but Christy Todd Whitman comes to mind when one considers the concept in its political context? And then there is the one I dare not name. My shame, my dark loveworker and tireless muscle of eros for whom all my degrees and intellectual achievements mean nothing. The one I worship in primitive passion. The one for whom I am not Puella Carpenter, girl dramaturg and lapsed feminist and disciple of Christy Todd Whitman, but only "Lou-Lou," passion's nightblooming cereus.

~

All of these several selves are jumbled about in a somewhat madcap, but wildly spontaneous manner, but without much plan or pretence. The *Moi*-theory of my old menteuse, Professor Rumple-Gneisenau's book *Miranda's Secret Aerial* allows for a ubiquity of grievance within the universal color-blind panopticon for unobstructed viewing of abuse, harassment, molestation, brutalization, rites of exclusion, silencing and erasure as a strategic mask-play in the oppositional grid that is the postmodernist's response to Phallocentric Patriarchy. This place is the site of my re-enactment of castration and the removal of my "thing" (Kristeva) by Phallocentric Logos. The contradictions I embody seek redress by, and from, the horrors of representation as I enact

Patriarchy's undoing—at work, at home, and in the very malls where I shop for lipstick, cue-tips and other telling (but useful) little items, ever alert to clues, apocope, the cynosure of my socially-constructed disappearance. I view my own torture, mutilation and dismemberment in the Panopticon with a dispassionate eye. Indeed, even at supposedly enlightened Molossus among my colleagues in the Women Studies Program, I found the encoded *ecriture* of mutilation and the death-rattle of the self's strangulation an everyday occurrence. Were it not for the videotape of my several angry meetings regarding my tenure with Professor Hilda Rumple-Gneisenau's own sister, Doctor Heidi Rumple-Basingstoke, the theorist of Bulimia-Ecriture, I could not have imagined such gross, brutish, buck-naked harassment. Naked, brutish and rampant. And on the part of a convicted woman, a self-confessed "helpless" heterosexual (like me). If the settlement with Molossus was less than what it surely should have been (the firm of Crosley, Doggo, Perigord and Balch skimmed off nearly a half, typical Late Capitalist swine); it nonetheless has enabled me to pursue the humble way of dramaturgy pretty much unensorcelled (by the demon of perennial need that haunts the campgrounds of non-profit-land). Looking back, I am saddened by the recent dual suicide of the two sisters; although I did wish therapy upon them at our last, unpleasant shouting match of a meeting across a marble table at the "Dove Descending" in Chenango Heights. Whatever the case, their fierce, vocal grievance was simply no match for the mountain of mine (studiously documented by all available contemporary mediums); for I was newer to the first bliss of my old traumatic discoveries, and so they resembled bright toys of my own invention—red wagon, toy cannon, dog with pink, fuzzy slippers—rather than complex, sedimented sites of phallocentric crime. The universal polyvocal sadomasochism of our sad, later capitalist tar-pit.

Theatre, I discovered happily, possessed no antibodies whatsoever to the virus of Critical Theory. My own sensitivity to the nuances of violation, abuse and the cryptogram of encoded ravishments would allow me free range in a world dominated by mild dreamers like Van Board, a person unable to hurt a flea; a man paralyzed easily (more easily even than academics, if that can be believed) by imagined or real pricks at the moral balloon of his sensitivity, a sensitivity filled with a rare and fragile Xenon. Or a notoriously short-lived Tritium of the soul.

~

And I wonder if I might, at this point in the streamline narrative I am pursuing, interject an aside on a subject that concerns me greatly, and which I may wish to take up later when the time comes for editing; I mean a whole chapter on the leering fullness of the moon, a force of diabolical urgency in all traditional literatures. Also the sign of womanhood in her mythical phase of abjection. Everywhere you go, it is obvious, unanalysable, a lethal truism. The moon as Raiser of the Tides, and the rough, gluey, fluid horror of our underselves; for the ultimate patriarchy may be lunar as well as solar and a fine piece of cosmic resentment. I do not trust the conventional

Luna, even when it hangs like a macabre, judging Micawber, grinning down at us from his perch in the sky. As I write, the moon's pale frisson bathes me in strangeness and in the horror of my abjection; I cannot stomach this and would rather bask in absolute darkness or the killing blight of Late Capitalist flourescence. The moon tries to remind me of the naked, histrionic cliches upon which this flesh is founded, upon which all that I aspire to become has, until now, foundered. Rendered a harmless commodity of calendar art by Western Man's harsh, seizing, starling gaze, the gaze that probes the sexual place, the gaze that would make a harem of an innocent elementary schoolyard such as the one I attended in subrural New Delbert, all too near (unknowingly so) the breadbasket of the tri-state area, New Baskets and its corrupt clan of Names. All of them, a ferocious primitive horde of Names, Names devoted to bashing, battering and abuse. All things weird, in Chris's pathetic description. So as the full moon leers down from his tower in the Father's night, so I close the shades and the shutters of my little Palmyran studio, and copy out these dramaturgical notes on the folly of summertime with Zenobian zest. But it is late, and in my weariness I digress; more of this later—my theory of lunar deconstruction.

14 [THE SPINE OF THE PLAY]:

To say I never imagined Chris capable of the crime he has, obviously, committed amounts to witless synechdoche. The artist is at heart a basically wicked creature, a cur, and the creative act itself always a violation, a transgression, a deed of enormous disruption and destructiveness. But I never supposed his demons would erupt in such an obviously horrific way. He seemed so sweet, in the mild midwestern way. Unfocussed and bland, harmless. Naive and restless, cute. I cannot imagine what his childhood was really like; for only on rare occasions was I able to get him to open up. If only for a little.

Weird, he said, Weird.

For starters it turned out my paternal grandfather and his paternal grandmother conducted a twenty year affair. They would meet at the Hotel Ajax in the slums of New Delbert, and consort with low-life types there. Desperados like Fats Bohannon, Joey the Bull and Madam Fortunato, all familiar figures from the annals of organized crime at the turn of the century. Like me, his submerged memory was full of bobbing scenes of casual, habitual abuse. Sodomy and buggery by aunts, uncles, and the lusty farm animals of more remote relations out on the prairies of New Baskets. For the truth was the Name clan was addicted to secret orgies where their young girls tested the sexual endurance of their brothers, fathers, fathers-in-laws, complaisant neighbors and the lusty farm animals. Before huge bonfires in the back yards of Palmyra and Athens, the dads and moms of that name would caress, fondle, copulate with, and bugger one another, and with the lusty farm animals they would howl, howl, howl beneath the summer moon. By day respectable folk, members of the Anaclastic branch of the Church of Christ the Risen. Owners of hardware stores, station wagons, cocker spaniels, and all tidy and zipped of lip. Like the country cousins of my own Carpenter line they feigned a certain suburban innocence, gullibility and tendency to mawkish dawdle. The barely perceptible quiver of the lip at the Pledge of Allegiance. Aunt Madge, so proud of her wolfish tomatoes. Saturnine

Glen, who wore straw hats. Henry, the pharmacist. Mickey, the insurance salesman. All of them, with names like Sue and Bill and Doody and Mell. Randy, with freckles and a paper route. Photo: Mell Name and Morris Name posed before the chicken coop in blue jeans, out up on the high western forty with Bobo the lab. No one at the 4H Club could have grasped the truth, nor at the PTA of New Delbert Elementary where Norbert Name presided, nor at the Lions Club of Rome where Lenny Name with his gap-toothed grin told his silly, apparently innocuous jokes. Lenny, the proud father of Emily, Susie and Lorna Doone, by Josie; three succotash blonds and their succotash mom, all apparently the most normal. And all tireless, driven fornicators, orgiasts and wantons. The bellowing and groaning of poor Chris's childhood. The twitching, parting of flesh and demoniac penetration of Name into, through and upon, other Names seemed almost beyond comprehension. The spilling eructation of Name upon Name. An anemone of tangled, incestuous copulations. Abuse beyond calculation, beyond chronicle—

that was young Chris's childhood, or so he hint-
ed to me over coffee at the Diner in Palmyra. It
was weird, he said, growing up.

That was the clue I needed. The affair between our respective grandpersons we deduced
by comparing collections of items from our respective familial attics, sites of memory, our odd
linked personal **shoah.** Collections of matchbox-
es, shoelaces, carnival tickets, receipts for dry
goods, singleton socks, hair clippings, hair-clips,
rings, earrings, pipe cleaners, hats, mouse drop-
pings and illegible love-letters, postcards, wilted
forget-me-nots, wreathes of red white and blue
ribbon, butterflies and unusual moths pinned to
wooden blocks or under glass, empty .22 car-
tridges, japanese beetle carcasses and June bugs,
blurred photos of young people with wild, transgressive eyes, bits of velours and what looked like
fur, fur. All suggestive of a violent collusion of
lusts, a collusion of lusts, the Auschwitz of our
innocence.

That was, indeed, weird.

~

My dissertation at the Groaner School of Drama provided me with much needed focus during the decade of so of my recovery. A place to be safe and to allow the bouncing ball of my trauma a respite from the old terror's cyclic reverb. Wise old Professor Glory was my friend and taught me much. His adaptations are deeply undervalued: Shakespeare's *Dog-hank* cycle, Chekhov's *Uncle Vaughn* (set in rural New Delbert), and Brecht's *Bon-vivant of Szechuan*. We live in a depressing, mediocre time, and the engine of rigor has been derailed, probably for the foreseeable future. And for all the futurisms beyond that. Van was one of the handful of artistic directors possessive of true vision, the spires and minarets of theatrical future beyond the bog of current pop-culture nihilism. Stand-up, language plays, the work of well-meaning (but inept) Africanocentrists whose work defies the precepts of the masters (Wuvorin comes to mind) and possesses no spine, no beginning, middle, or end—and certainly no catastasis. Only plays with backbone, buttressed by an Inner

Dream are able to fully elucidate the dark bird of trauma, and come clean in an eructive whoosh of confession and self-revelation. So when I consider the sad events of the last days, of poor dismembered Van, and of poor deluded Chris I can only think back to those happy days at Groaner, and Wuvorin's masterful *Cheese of Baghdad*, the finest show I ever saw there.

Such clarity and singleness of dramatic action; such unencumbered drive, dynamism and univocal duodenism (the three D's of Swanhope's great theoretical study The Floating City: Wuvorin's "cheez" and the Annihilation Effect). The greatest intellects at Groaner recalled the classical cloud-seeding of minds at Athens and Pergamun; not to mention the Bohemian dives of West Chenango where the Supernaturalist School met in ouijian conviviality, hosted by the brave-hearted Luther T-Burbank Moss and Bobby Cantrell whose *Amazing Floss,* with its stark, unsentimental portrayal of life at the Junior Dental College of Whitlow revolutionized local playwriting, and especially the Buccal-Realist School; and of course, one must not forget *Secrets of a Sunken*

Mall, first of a long series of poetical dramas by the playwright laureate John "Flatfish" Dory, who much later authored the Wurlitzer Prize winning *Ovarian Melodies* and the Tambo-musical *Darkness at Midnight.* These wild, artistic souls, and many more, studied with both Glory and Swanhope at Groaner during the salad days of Dean Harrison Hennigan Bun. But Camelots are fleeting phenomenons, alas. This genius of fund-raising and aggressive marketing, who could read Wuvorin and *Monsieur Moonbox* in their own languages (Moonbox being Basque) suffered a long, lubricous decline owing to a wrongly diagnosed variant of Mad Cow Disease (Lesson: always wash hands after feeding your tropical fish) called Rothko's Truffle-Mold Morbula, which destroys only the neural centers governing moral and aesthetic discrimination. How terrible it must have been for this most fastidious of all arts administrators to find himself becalmed in an oily Sea of Bad Taste, condemned to tell frequently filthy, unfunny jokes about the "Art of the Fart" and Jesus Fornicator (bizarrely reminiscent of that site-specific atrocity, Herr N's *Circle*

Jerk for the Saviour and Twelve Rutting Rabbis).
But true lovers of the theatre always supported,
and always honored his occasionally daedelian
choices. For Bun was a true classicist and knew
that nothing current possesses anything approaching the wattage of the ancients: Sophocles,
Aeschylus and the lost dramas of Dromion, not
to mention the fragmentary theatrical land-mines
of Mnesychryssonippus. Alone of our dramatists
Madelaine Mower may be mentioned alongside
these bright beacons; her *Fist of God* comes to
mind, although the quaint, sentimental device of
resurrection by backhoe (the young girl-harlot-
priestess of Boron has flung herself into the
Tarpit of Melancthon to avoid Pharaoh's caress-
es, you will recall) only highlights the chronic il-
logic of the contemporaneous. The ancient Illyrian masters saw more clearly that life is no bowl of
cherries, as in Dromion's version wherein Perfec-
ta is not dredged up from the mire, her white
breast mired in adhesive bitumen. Rather, she
finds peace in sticky death. The cult that springs
from her calamity washes the wounds of the city's
rape (Meteoron) till late in Byzantine days, be-

fore Michael Ducas Angelus Comnenus, that rabid nominalist, confiscates their building as a hospital for his drunken band of brigands in 1333.

But such clarity and singleness of dramatic action is not now in vogue. Neither in the precinct of the art, nor in the hurly-burly of contemporary life, art's counterfeit. My own difficult progress in early career offers a case to point to. Before Great Wind, I interned at Gogol Rep, apparently a wise thing to do. Who knew? Who knew what dangers there were, slouching and lurking about in dark passageways, at that solemn, respectable tortoise-hulk of a theatre? For an experience soon befell me there, strange, like a three-legged race under the dark of the moon rising up against the red-tide, of an unholy descending escalator. And a weird, unimaginable moonrise I would grow to rue. It happened a little like this.

During my junior year abroad I studied classics at Tubingen, with a certain Professor Cermak, from someplace in Eastern Europe. I do believe Connie knows his work, which except for the small book *On Blight,* remains untranslated— and presumably untranslatable—owing to certain peculiarities of his Perfidian idiolect. Cermak and I became lovers, and through him I met, aside from the figure of my dark disaster, the eminent stage theorist of the late Deutches EnSemble (DES) one Herr Odwalla, a genius. Odwalla was my first genius in fact, and the most forceful and aggressive dramaturg imaginable. His disdain for the contemporary lifted him entirely out of the contemptible world of ordinariness. In Odwalla's view (developed in concert with Cermak's Radical Pessimism) the shallow and totalistic world of Late Capitalist text must be subverted by intrusion of transgressive **Ur-**, or PreText; simultaneously, it must be rendered morbid by repeated injection of PostTextual venom—theory. Classics in decisive adaptation (rebundled, in Odwalla's terminology) are to be reconceived as weapons, Tools for Cultural Pay Back, in order to accentuate the litotic-hyperbolism of the Historic West's tragic sigilliaroid. All this was not so easy for me to understand, but my colleagues among the radical young Greens welcomed me, and helped me on the thornier issues. I joined their nudist societies and beer clubs. We visited Holderlin's tower and the place—I forget—where that ingenuous nut Celan embarrassed the Magician of Messkirch with his rude reply. Cermak and Odwalla took me to a quaint reunion of the latter's family deep in the gothic interior of the Schwarzwald: men in their old war uniforms (jet black and stylish) weaved to and fro in their BMW wheelchairs, drank the local brew *Blaubartsbier,* and waved their aluminum prostheses at one another as they reminisced, talking of Stalingrad and the Kursk Salient—things that escaped me, things from the world of ordinariness that I knew not. But to my mind Theory and Theoretical Historicity has quite rendered tedious facticity a thing of the past. Let history be drowned in its own bog. But then, I am an American at heart (my girlish good-looks are one of my strong points), and so this is the way you would expect me to regard such things. I always plan to look younger than I am.

I can still see the bright vision of myself, smiling in my huge American way, when Odwalla asked me to be assistant dramaturg on the remount of Von Teufel's legendary production of

Traubel's *Trochilidae*, itself transmogrified during the Enlightenment from the ancient Illyrian of Dolichopus. Wow, I said, barely able to make my tongue work in my cheek.

15 [THE FOCUS MOVES TO A WOMAN
WRITING: YOU ARE THE MODEL...
THE EVENT IS YOU:

But how long, under such circumstances, can one
resist the omnipotence of the despotic gaze? I
succumbed to Herr Odwalla, for he seemed to
me at the time to be the ultimate, Nordic 'turg.
In Luneberg, Kiel and Peenemunde, I worked as
the piece deepened, thickened and grew heavy
with gloomy, theatrical portent. And twice as
vivid. Van Teufel's endlessly iterated shriek,
"Nein, nein" and "Das ist Scheisse" haunted my
dreams, just as it reverberated in all my working
hours. True, I was treated more or less contemp-
tuously, almost as a "Revuegirl" rather than as a
person of ideas, a somebody to be reckoned with.
Still, I did imagine my time would come; indeed,
that when the show was to be remounted at
Molossus the following year, I with my vast experience of the European tour, not to mention language skills and profound insight into the prob-

lems of catastasis, would emerge swan-like from my lowly ducklinghood, my apprenticeship as *Das Entschen* and step forth in full dramaturgical bloom. Alas, it was not to be.

For Von Teufel turned out to be a cynical and devious roue, famously adept at playing off contenders for his limited peripheral attention. To my horror, once we had established ourselves in the Palmyra Days Inn and reported for our first North American run-through, I was shocked to behold there; there in the wide, nearly endless loop or oval of chairs (the rehearsal hall was vast, probably an old airplane hangar), aside from actors, directors, assistant directors, stage manager, assistant stage managers, designers of all kinds, their associates, agents and assistants; not to mention a crowd of interns, observers, curious board members, flunkies, toadies, leather boys and girlfriends of the various personages involved; but there, at Odwalla's side a chair, yes an empty chair that was to be reserved (so I was informed by the second assistant stage manager's assistant, the third assistant prop boy) for a continuous rotation, in succession, of all the dramaturgs, recent and historical, of any renown or even passé, over the hill and totally discredited from the entire region, New Delaware and New Baskets included. Was I ever shocked. Indeed, within a few moments who should appear but my hated rival from Groaner days, Jonathan Peter Michael, a fawning swine responsible for spreading some particularly vicious innuendoes about me and my predilection for all things black and use of mousse. Once more I felt as if confined to Bentham's Panopticon so rigorously problematized by Foucault in his memorable book, a book I confess to have lightly skimmed in certain, terrifying places.

In future weeks, during the slow and agonizing rehearsal process ("Scheisse! Scheisse!"), I was put upon with every conceivable humiliation and temporizing half-measure in order to situate myself closer and closer to **the chair;** to the chair in question because I knew it to be, in a sense, the essential chair. The Platonic chair; chair **qua** chair. So once I had wheedled, whined and wiggled my way to its vicinity I waxed ecstatic, because it had become evident to all, even Von

Teufel himself and my mentor Odwalla, that I was not about to be denied. I would become co-dramaturg for this American production of Odwalla's version of Trauble's by way of Dolichopus willy nilly. In coy and sexy tones I insinuated my way into the great men's talk. For they were wholly innocent of Wuvorin's theories of catastasis, and in especial the topic of my dissertation at Groaner, post-catastasis; clearly my ideas on this and other theoretical matters were bound to break open the kernel, the very nut of Dolichopus/Traubel/Odwalla's postmodern *chef du theatre*.

But, just as my plan seemed to reach a fruitful culmination, disaster struck. I arrived one day for rehearsal, as usual a little late because I had been up quite late the night before preparing notes on the trope of the hummingbird in some of Dolichopus's attic rivals, notably Mnopius and Pnander, both prolific writers of the partly obscene, partly atrotropaic theatrical persiflage so popular at the time. The hummingbird as Virgin/Whore (T. Pudenda); the hummingbird as swaggering braggart (Trochilodus Gloriosus);

the hummingbird as slimy money-changer
(Trochilidus Penurium); and lastly, the hummingbird as ithyphallic sexual and political proto-
tyrant: Trochilidus Rex. It was always my custom
to come prepared for any eventuality, particularly
in the case of a potentially complex situation; this
was Glory's rule at Groaner. Thus, you can imagine my chagrin as I entered the vast, gloomy am-
phitheater, whiffling past the gang of leering
techies with their incessant hoots, wolf-whistles
and hard, knowing sexual gazes; rushed on, the
rapid, little-girl steps that had been my perambu-
latorial signature since childhood, and during
those wonderful summers at Camp Wampus
Wampus in the Delores Mountains of North
New Fracture. Arriving at the site where all of us
assistants—assistants directorial and assistants
stage managerial and our assistant assistants—
were accustomed to lurk, whisper and make other
sounds like that of crumpled paper in the dusty
half-light, I could see with a sinking feeling in my
craw, that there was a person seated in my chair.
Yes, this was true. Back and forth I slithered
among the crowd of lesser actors in their fezzes

and bizarre Illyrian gowns, frippery, baubles and rings of chryselephantine, past toadies and flacks, past hangers-on and the marketing people with their glazed, dead eyes, past Molossus's lesser Deans and arts administrators from the State Art Council and the Moses and Aaron Reventlow Foundation, a major funder of projects like this; squinting, tilting my head to peer over shoulders and between whispering shadows I determined there could be not a doubt. There was a person, a squat, lank Germanic-type person in my seat, my seat! and a black leather jacket flung upon its back, a jacket rather like the ones I had seen in the Black Forest that day, the one worn by Odwalla's charming uncle, Wolfius. Only this one was of the finest lambskin, buttery soft and of such a quick and slippery and titillative sensuousness that my fingers reached out to touch, to touch, to touch its butteriness almost without my volition. Even from a distance its thuringian butteriness could be almost savored. This could only be one person: the legendary Grundschlamm, dramaturg of dramaturgs. Grundschlamm, the **Ur**-dramaturg whose dense, riddling pittle-pattle was so difficult none but the most erudite could fathom it. Reportedly, both Derrida and Foucault left baffled and shaken after an audience, years ago, with Grundschlamm. Nowadays no one dared to talk to the master except through his factotum, Lindwurm. Lindwurm, the "Dragon of Dusseldorf." Back at Groaner I had of course attempted to scale the heights of Grundschlamm's masterpiece *Uber Hesychasm,* a work to set aside the *Tractatus,* or Cermak's pal's *Being and Time.* Alas, the book was way beyond my powers and I plummeted, I toppled from its heights down into the dense foliage of its foothills, intimidated, abashed and psychically bruised. Now Von Teufel's assistant's assistant's intern was whispering in my ear. Van Teufel was screaming ("Nein, nein") at the chorus of crows, so I had to ask the intern to repeat herself. You've been replaced, she hissed—Heidi was her name; was this karma? She explained, Odwalla needs someone to focus on the meso-catastasis of the third act. Stunned, I simply leaned against the wall. Odwalla yelped his fierce yelp, and the young girl leapt from me back to his side.

So, for a long time I simply leaned against the wall, numbed by my catastrophe. For I had never, ever dreamed such a thing could happen; my preparation had been like the over-production of corn the region has traditionally been known for: useless, silly, and strangely, strangely unavoidable. I slapped my forehead with the heel of my hand: yes, yes, yes, of course, the meso-catastasis; now it was all clear. How could I have been so stupid, so intellectually naive? The spiny, pricklish feeling we all (Van Teufel and Odwalla both, and all our assistants and assistant's assistants) had dimly sensed and alluded to only haltingly…ah hah! It had all been a question of meso- rather than post-catastasis; and so all my training was for nought. Only a genius like Grundschlamm could have seen through, with laser-precision, to identify the point of our halting confusion, our "ah hums" and "hmms" and "ynghns" and so forth. So now there was simply nothing for it, but to leave. Me, leave. And so I did. In silence, and in the despondent depths of dejection. Abject dejondency. crap-headed blear. Gooner tubed as we used to say at Camp Wampus-Wampus, after one of us had failed to nork the flag, at the deep end of the pool.

With no place to call my own, with no place to sit, I experienced my full humiliation under the hegemonic aegis of the Universal Signifier. Shudderingly naked, for all to view, in Odwalla's Panopticon. Like a madwoman I flew madly about, and out the revolving door; flew scowling and scuttering like a large, very angry bird. A pelican perhaps, an evil mock Wolf-Egret of mammoth proportion, or a cenozoic egg-sleeking Diatryma with a horny bill capable of breaking heads. In short, a fearsome thing. I ensconced myself at the nearby Westside Diner, a hangout popular among the more oafish variety of frat boy. I ordered a dry martini.

Three days later I woke up, half-clothed, at the ATO house in Whitlow with a frightening hangover and a new set of values. Suddenly I could see the point of risk-aversion, and why it is so crucial to the American theatre. Larry and Toby and Lewis, my young friends at ATO prepared a massive breakfast of ham and eggs and listened respectfully as I went off again and again, on the subject of Germans, dramaturgy and German dramaturgy. Being pre-med and pre-law students, they had not a clue what I was talking about, the fools. I think they imagined I was some kind of academic amateur archeologist. Babbling older woman, though looking younger than her age, haloed with a nimbus of extremely angry golden locks. The kind of unusually evolved woman one only finds on campuses in places like New Delbert where the circles of rustic, subrural abuse and hegemonic logophallic hierarchy intersect and situate scandals of the sort I am recounting.

But let me waste no more time on Grandschlamm, nor on that parasitical creep Lindwurm. Van Renssalaer Board, two years ahead of me at Groaner, responded to my resume and hired me on the spot for Great Wind. My new career, as play mechanic and enthusiast for the then newly emerging New American Play industry (NAPs) was, therefore, launched. I would forswear the poisoned apple of the international Avant Garde with its hype, pretension and backbiting intrigue for the more manageable and earth-bound world of American-type developmental theatre. Had not Wayland "Wink" Frich (brother to Wank) started here, with *White Sands* and *Things Seen in Morocco's Mirror;* not to mention, *Norm Best's fabulous Lord of Toads* and *Tony's Accidental Eating of Bugs?* Van and I got along well, a definite plus. He had just replaced "Mad Daddy" Moonbrick as Artistic Director after the latter's production of Jack Crowe Daw's *A Hand-grenade for My Father* proved the last (jack) straw for the Rep's tight-fisted board. Highfalutin piffle, according to Board President Linda Yaddo Darkwood, heiress to the Wah Wah Whiskey fortune, and founder of the valuable New Delbert Institute of Upper Colonics. (Jack Daw, that ironic creep; his wiseacre *A Gold Candle for a Black Camel* with its send-up of Professor Glory's and Swanhope's credo wasn't nearly so smart as he thought; I confess I was the one who ratted, and got him thrown out of Groaner. I hate these literary playwrights who think they are so smart their plays don't need fixing; these guys [and they are always guys] who imagine Daedalus was more than a man with wings.)

152

After Jake Hall's brief stint as interim Artistic Director, Van got the job, partly because (at my velvety suggestion) he promised the Board. Oh yes, promised the Board that Great Wind's programming would no longer fly in the face of community values, societal values, family values, societal values in general—and whatever other values might be of value to the entrepreneurial big shots and high rollers who bank-rolled the Rep. Solid folk who wanted a solid, risk-averse classical repertoire; those who confined their risk-taking to the fine art of money-making. And after my dire catastrophe at the hands of the international Avant Garde, the phony PC faggot avant-garde, who could complain? Rock the boat? Kvetch? Surely not me. And I, thus, quickly learned that Promising Playwrights (like young playwrights and imprisoned ones), like most of the abjected of the region—New Delaware, New Dumbo and New Baskets—were a lot easier to deal with. They generally didn't know much about theatre; and even better: they didn't talk back. Which brings me to the subject of Chris. Christian W. Name. Poor, poor Chris.

16 [ON THE LEERING FULLNESS OF THE MOON]:

Moon. Maan. Man…. The dream of a person, elfin I, hegemonically erased and thus reduced to an epistemic trace by an act of violent mutilation on the part of the Universal Signifier. What can I say? I go on, alone, under the leering fullness of the moon. I suppose I should have known the price I would pay for my fateful passion, and the stickle-prickle of its lascivious play, and sway. My spring break in Perfidia that year, 79 or 83 or whatever, the year of the King of Autumn in Tamar, the year of my thesis on the Medieval House of Lingerie and its mini-theatre at Druve, where I first met Connie—Constantine Ducas Angelus Kurcak, now my dearest friend at the Rep and the architect of my undoing; it was Connie who brought to me that daedal masterwork, the hebdomad chronicle of Uuc, Uuc in the full frenzy of his hebephrenia, leering in his fullness like the blazing cream porcelain of the moon. And with it dear Thorny, the dead letter of my broken, broken heart. For it was Thorny's great-great-great great granddaddy, Prince Casimir Thornley the Mirific, who purchased the single battered manuscript of *Q's Q* consisting of the hebdomad (seven) books of fine-lettered Turko-Tungusic, four thousand pages—each the stretched, cured and oiled wing of the Giant Perfidian Plum Barbastel, a frugivorous bat; or, a flying box of a fox—from General Godart Van Ginkel, friend to William of Orange and Legate to the Paleologii, in their humiliating exile at Genoa. Prince Thornley's secret treasure was passed down, Thorn by Thorn, to the louche deceiver who became my "dark demon." But there are things, deep things of the heart and soul which cannot be reckoned in the pathetic language of Late Capitalism, that flat jazz. It was Thorny himself whom I suspect masterminded the whole fiasco of Constantine's phoney visa, the theft of which led, albeit obscurely, to the subsequent terrorist debacle of Pannair Flight 677 blown out of the skies above startled Chenango; and the whole creepy flourish of charges, countercharges; the TV crews and shameless appropriation of the tragedy by politicians, in especial, Senator Slim Slenderer, Republican fruitcake out of Vacaville and Senator Moses "High Tops" Kellogg, that beet-faced Chairman of Ways and Means, a perennial supporter of foreign aid to Perfidia, and a man capable of anything stickle-haired or stickle-mickle, according to columnist Susie Sunday, my pal at the Athens *Torpedo,* the only respectable newspaper in the region.

~

And now I feel so alone, exiled and alone out on the prairies of New Delbert, New Dumbo, Palmyra and the whole wheaten swath of roly-poly New Baskets. No one understands my cold and difficult nature. The moon with its leering face monitors my slipping sense of consequence and self-possession. I yield slowly into theatrical alterity and excess. Van's dead. After the incident involving the late Professors H and H at Molossus I am not exactly the Belle of the ball in those stucco'd and ivy-choked halls. My dark demon lurks far off in Tamar, except for his rare visits to

New York and Chenango, where he takes in the fabulous autumns we are known for. But he is no longer attentive to me, his "slut muffin," nor to my noctilucent needs. I look into the mirror of my dreary little flat and wonder darkly what it all means. I still own that quizzical, rabbit-poised-for-a-fast-getaway look that drove some men mad; still stand five foot three and tip the scales at a hundred and three; the iris-miracle of my transcendental yellowhair has not faded into the dust of commonplace ordinariness—and yet, and yet. I cannot put my finger on it, but something feels different, something I was possessed by without knowing fully, without knowing what it was has fled, flown and fluvio-vacuated…and I do not know what to do. I have all my life walked the wide circle, within the compass of what I thought winnable. In the name of what I believed in, or what is the same: what I thought it appropriate to believe in. Isn't that enough, I ask myself, and find this same tiresome self tumbling down an infinite regress. Something about my choices reminds me of my old habit of returning to places where I have suffered too tellingly ever to speak in full voice. It is as if I have allowed no one into the rabbit hole of my fateful passion. Although I am a witness to all the horrific depredation of these times I am allowed to witness, I feel a disquieting sense that no one is interested very much in me, or in what I think, or say, or do. That, in fact, what I think or say or do is a pretty dull and empty affair and that even my affairs of the heart, the flirtations with Van, Connie and poor Chris, for example, are all so much smoke and odorless gas—meaningless and passionless guesses at something genuinely human or instrumental. I feel the dead hand of the ages guiding me, career and heart both; that even my inner colloquy is purposeless, undirected, vague, hollow, pompous and utterly without conviction, passion, direction, guts, or...spontaneity. I watch myself at all moments. Watch myself perform, and fail to perform. Exceed my span and recalibrate the part of me that sets the measure for the next act, whether of thought, deed or speech, so that I may exceed that; or not, as the case may be. It is all the same, all a series of bright, flashing, astonishing, and extremely impressive disappointments, disappointing figments of the soul. So that as I consider what must I do what must I do what must I do, there is nothing that comes to mind, comes to mind with any certainty. I look up from the deep and familiar confines of my rabbit hole and view not a small circle of infinity, a small circle bespeckled with a manageable array of star, no, no, hardly; I look up and what caps the top of my rabbit hole, my own personal rabbit tunnel, is the leering face of the moon.

~

Dear, dearest Thorny: Even though I am abjected and possessed of a ruined soul, there is enough left in me of me to do this one act of rejection. Especially after the horrible dismemberment of poor Van I can see how brief our candles' burn is. No more shall I shepherd the fruits of your Perfidian genius through the flaming hoops of American developmental theatre. It is simply not worth it. Find someone else to dramaturg *Q's Q*. I never really liked it anyway. Something about the story, something about the spine of it always gives me the prickles. Like the scary narratives and nightmarish tales Connie insists on sharing with me. Flying, murderous forks and walking cannibal houses. Oh, enough. Maybe I'll even try writing my own play. Only, what shall I call it? What.... Moon. Maan. Man. The story would be one of a person hegemonically erased and...

V: Jake

17 [IN THE MIDDLE OF MY MIDDLE PASSAGE]:

In the middle of my Middle Passage I encountered the she-wolf, the she-wolf of hatred. I did not turn away, I held to my course and prevailed, for that she-wolf was the Chair Woman of the Board of Directors of Great Wind Repertory, one of the whitest institutions among all the institutional theatres in the tri-state area, Lydia Yaddo Darkwood. This was at the time of Artistic Director "Mad Daddy" Moonbrick's decent into outright insanity. I had never angled or politicked for the job because, to be frank and fair to myself, I did not want to. I did not need to. After my string of hits in Chenango, beginning with *As Phalt Brotherz* I knew that, given the political opportunity, I could do no wrong. Perfect Prentiss's feature on **petit moi** in the *Torpedo* established me as the single most-influential African-American in the performing arts since... since...the so-called *"Bronze Venus,"* Lena Horne, that oreo (whom I lampooned in an early piece by that name—*Bronze Venus*). My black fanny was one hotter than hot butt, and I took care to keep up the momentum. Go for the ride, my mother always said. Go take it to them where they live, said Riley Dogg Potts, my mentor and only master, now Emeritus at Chenango State.

So this Darkwood lady was not doing anything but what she had to; the Rep was in a dizzy free-fall ever since the death of Sidney Yellin, its founder. I knew she hated me because her class all do. But the time has come when they need us more than we need them. Hire the famous coon, I can hear them say. Yeah, and he's gay to boot so we've covered our bases. Yeah, if he was a Jew he'd be nigh on perfect. But I am no Jew; I'm an Abyssinian redactor, a song and dance man of the first order. When I get done with American theatre you will not recognize the place, because the face of it will have changed. Somewhere, I know, my ancestors are proud of me, proud at how I have seized my chance to right some wrongs that can, properly speaking, never be righted. Because the white liberals think I'll settle for half a loaf, and sit quietly at Ole Massa's table while they glow in the radiation of their self-congratulation. Only they got another think coming. And that is a fact because I have a real agenda. So after being interim AD I turned them down. I didn't need it. But it looks like the job's open again. Poor, dumb Van. Life's a wheel.

And now? Time goes on, and with it the realization that nothing much can truly, or does really, ever change. We are always lost in the retreat of time from the point of immediacy. A hundred years from the destruction of the old plantation system even, and what in the way of real transformation has that century brought? The status quo changes cosmetically, but even that barely. I am an instrument that belongs to the silenced voices of my ancestors, and am of their will. It is why I shall be heard. Their voices speak truths. Towering truths and deep submerged ones that are tricky and hard to understand. Those white women at the foundations always have a hard time with deep, submerged things like truth. You have to point out to them as clearly as possible that they are the great-grandchildren and great-great-grandchildren of the most appalling racists who have ever walked the face of the earth. North and South together, both of them in on it, sure. The Civil War was not fought to free the black man, period. The Civil War was not fought to free the black man, but to preserve the Union. You can look that up. You can look that up because the illusion that anyone really intended to demolish the engine of slavery is just that, an illusion. Western society has always been a tissue of such constructed illusions, veil behind veil. An edifice of unreal and frequently monstrous fictions. We African-Americans have had to learn how to perceive and comprehend the basic set-up for what it is, through the veils. Through the illusory veils and shifting mirages. Slavery had to be reconstructed as Reconstruction. Then it had to be reconstructed as Plessy vs Ferguson Booker T. Washington up by the bootstraps Sambo temporizing. And why did it have to be reconstructed? Because as an ethical system it did not obtain. The face of slavery did not like itself, and the bucket from which it drew water did not hold water. I am not, you understand, saying that my ancestors died in vain. They live on in me, and I am their full, historical justification. I am both their justification and signification because every show I direct amounts to a doing of the dozens, with respect, upon our ancestral themes. You will notice I add "with respect." This "with respect" is crucial because the present is only an extension of the past, like a riff by Miles into the unknown construction of the future. It would perhaps be too crude, in this context, to call this present present something like "payback time"; too crude, but apt.

~

After the success of *Bronze Venus,* my searing expose of that super-kinky oreo, Lena Horne, I bought a little condo in a posh corner of Bromley Heights and a summer place out near Palmyra. Van I encountered, I seem to recall, some eight years back at a theatre conference in, was it Molossus, Princeton or Whitlow? We discussed bringing *Venus* to the Rep but nothing ever came of it. And why, really, would I want to bother with some cracker podunk anyhow? But I ended up doing some developmental work on *Black **Im** Black* at the Rep; one thing led to another, and I agreed to do a reading or two. In fact, I proposed a series of Plays That Kick: Tomorrow's Plays Today on the African-American Experience. Well, MacDonalds had the same damn problem with their awards program in New York. I warned Van it would happen again if he wasn't really careful, but he promised no, no, no, it couldn't happen again. The Selection Committee was aware of the problem, and that it would be a foregone conclusion that the recipient would be one of us, meaning one of you (meaning one of us). Van's the kind of white boy Artistic Director who drives me crazy. Pony tail, small white boy-type beard. Black leather jacket from C. K. Wang's in Chenango. Basically your grown-up mall-rat who thinks the Blues is where it's happening. So when he showed me the winning scripts, two of them, I smelled a rodent of major proportion. Both by a jerk named Name. Now the first took place on Mars. Van, my dear, no person of color would write a play that takes place on Mars. Mars is not on the multicultural agenda because science fiction is the last redoubt of the sons and daughters of the Confederacy. In outer space you can fill up your fictions with darkeys and call 'em "Squonks" or "Neezils." The agenda remains the same. A racial hegemony disguised as something else, something cool. I am not an idiot.

And the second one, even worse, was called *Q's Q.*

All this Cuman shit, and *Q's Q* is no more than some damn demented code for a predictable and racialist redaction. Cumans are the cracker author's stand-ins for niggas. And what does Mars have to do with the African-American experience? Yeah but the part on earth all takes place in Harlem and Chenango Heights, he says, and the depictions are so life-like and colorful. And of course the guy does end up being you know what, despite what Van promised. White bread as white bread can be: this Name jerk, a jerk. Also, I could have told him: No black person is named Christopher. Your average Christopher is either a fairy or a Christian Scientist.

~

So I reluctantly agreed to direct one of the readings, anyway and people came and when the shouting started I decided it was time to depart. I have a reputation to maintain. Dumb-ass play. Both of them one long blue in my head. I refuse to take responsibility for someone else's misguided notion of what constitutes art. The white man has lost his mind. Flying forks and such shit just do not cut it, I told Van on the way out. I knew he was on the way out too, though he did not. I was and am still negotiating with the Board of Directors on the details.

When I heard about the murder I was not, I'll admit, too surprised. Pestilential scum will be pestilential scum, and what goes around comes around. Ice-people got to do what they got to do, and that ain't my kind of funk.

Another project of mine, fabulous, came from a suggestion of Supervilious Johnson, who is chief hired coon at WPOO in Rome. Smart guy, Super, but when push comes to shove just another Tom. The best class of Tom, but a Tom nevertheless. Same old up by the bootstraps philosophy that marks the classic Tom. But even a Tom has a good idea every once in a blue moon. I am too terrific in my own fabulous self-regard to be intolerant of another man's jive, especially if that other man is a person of color. So, we were enjoying ourselves over veal marsala at The Sensitive Plant, a very swish joint in Domely, when he mentions the little known fact there was, in fact, an all black regiment of American volunteers enlisted in the German S.S. during the Second World War. No shit. This is true. Super is the kind of guy that digs up stuff like this, dark wicked stuff like this. Tragically, the entire outfit was exterminated, along with their commander *Obersturmfuhrer* George Washington Davenport, on April 15th, 1945 in the Russian assault on the Seelow Heights. I got so excited by the thought of all those brave, young African-Americans, sleek and sexy in their black and silver S.S. duds, I could barely contain myself; soon as I got back home I was sketching out a plan for the first act of what would become *Black **Im** Black,* a new-style pomo spectacle with song and dance. Yolanda Carlos, that asp at the *Torpedo,* had the temerity to question the ethical implications of the venture so I made sure she did no more dramaturging at the Rep, nor at Gogol Rep. Nor at any other recognized Rep of any size in the tri-state region. The truth is, as the philosopher wrote, my enemy's enemy is my friend; and the United States military is, and always has been, a total cracker outfit. So I perceive a deeper justice in the whole thing. If only these tough fighters (members of the crack 20th Panzer Grenadiers) had, at least once, the opportunity to engage their true foes on the western front my design would have been perfect. Still, facts will be facts, so I did not see any point in getting gummed up with correcting technicalities. And, as everybody knows, the Slavs are among the most ferocious racists to be found anywhere. Witness their sense-less slaughter of the entire Cuman people (a.k.a. niggas, you will recall) all on a single day. Some-where back in the olden times. The metaphor could be turned in various angles, to reveal both the basics of race-pride, and our intrinsic power-ful sexiness. The profound sexiness of blood and steel. Thus I both cash in on the notably news-worthy, and create a scandalously fabulous and pretty much impossible to criticize (by the un-trumpable first rule of abjection) piece of highly accessible showcraft. Wank Frich sings to my tune, baby, along with the discerning few, very few but an important few, it must be admitted, among white women of note in the vestibules of higher cultural journalism. Like Perfect Prentiss, who has compared me to the Twenties. Not to a mere mortal, but to an epic of excellence, ele-gance and sophistication. And all of it wrapped up in a single, rather adroit individual, me.

~

The way I see it, things at the Seelow Heights must have gotten drastic those last few days. The

173

main Russian artillery barrage began at 3am on the 14th. Five hundred million pounds of explosives in the first half-hour. Marshall Zhukov had this bright idea, as part of the initial assault: his troops would shine bright searchlights ahead of them, thus blinding the German defenders. But very quickly this all backfired as the light reflected, back, off the smoke of the exploding shells and blinded the advancing Russians themselves. Topographically speaking the Seelow Heights aren't all that impressive; just a wedge of sand dunes a little over two hundred meters high and fifteen kilometers long, running rough north to south. But the Germans had dug themselves in pretty thoroughly, camouflaged and buried their tanks to make their lines both invisible and unbreachable. Also, the German line of fire was angled down at 45 degrees allowing them to easily rake the lumbering Russian columns below, which quickly got fouled up, stalled and blocked by their own comrades as vehicle after vehicle was destroyed or damaged. For a time the engagement seemed a savage, one-sided turkey-shoot, with the white man taking it on the chin. Something like 30,000 Russians died in those early attacks. On the next day, however, the weather cleared and Zhukov called in his Stormoviks to pulverize the German positions. Because Marshall Z wanted badly to be the first to arrive and, hopefully, take Berlin; but to the south his rival Konev was approaching the German capital, racing across open terrain almost unopposed. The only thing standing in Zhukov's way was a couple of battered S.S. brigades including the 20th Panzer Grenadiers, along with a few hundred black asses in Davenport's regiment. This is the fatal flashpoint that ignites into a torch-song for the show, and its apotheosis also. For, by the end of the following night they were all dead. They were all dead, but they had fought heroically against impossible odds, fought for race-pride with gallantry, resoluteness and extraordinary bravery. This story, so long neglected, may only be one of many, but to me it epitomizes everything my ancestors would have me give voice to, if we possess a telephone to the grave, as I do fervently believe.

Why would I want to run Great Wind Repertory, that white woman Darkwood queried through pale, thin lips and narrow hate-filled eyes. The more she and her cheesy liberal-assed colleagues flattered me the more I felt the engine of their hate.

Because, I said, and the undertow of what I said was probably a little different from what I actually did say because you have to talk all that safe talk about "community" and "affirmative action" and "groups unrepresented in the profession" and such even while you know all of it, the entire shebang, is just window-dressing. And the undertow was this: To make up for every outrage committed against me and my people by you and your people, running back to the days of the prophets and the pharaohs; back to the days of our saviour, Osiris, who was torn limb from limb, yes, torn limb from limb by his white brother from the Ice-kingdom far to the north, near the North Pole, near the North Pole where the devil lives in his unholy mists and fogs, plotting and farting and conniving against all who live and prosper, who sing and follow the rule of the most ancient ones, close by Mareotis in the Nile delta;

and he who set upon the task of murdering Osiris, his own brother, I am talking dog-faced Seti, the true type of the Antichrist and an incarnation of the fiend himself, a moneychanger and a moneylender, an overseer and slave-master, a whore-monger and vicious swine-eating bully who has, time and time again, usurped the lore and traditions of others and made them over in his own foul and despicable image. So there, sitting opposite me at the conference room of Great Wind Repertory Theatre I, through the ineradicable double vision, double vision of the color-line, a double vision bequeathed to me by my ancestors through the language of the forest and of the drum, through the voices that whisper to me out of the swirling Frankincense, deep essential voices speaking to me, through me, in Yoruban and in Ibo and in Congolese of Black Isis, the boy goddess who is my protector, and who appeared in a fiery halo amid the ranging searchlights at the foot of the Seelow Heights that morning in 1945, like the dream of that old Roman whore-monger and slave-driver Constantine, at the battle of whatever: IN HOC SIGNO

VINCES. By whatever means necessary. And that brilliantly, shiningly ebony boy showed the way and directed a torrent of flame and steel, flame and steel from the whining 88's to the booming of the half-buried Tigers, down, down upon the crude and hapless Russian ofays, trapped each in the hot steel of his solipsistic cold-hearted solitary doom. Black Isis, as fabulous as the voice in the whirlwind that that African-American and our Moses of Moseses, Riley Dogg Potts, has also heard (in his mind), at Seelow, looking down.

19 [BLACK ISIS]:

But let me back away from the awful visage of the Typhonian Animal, Setuthu; it is too appalling to contemplate for long, and I am after all a man of the theatre. When I look in the mirror, however, I catch sight of a wholly other destiny, a destiny that is truly of our time, and of and through the better class of funding community—The Natchez and Flora P. Swayback Foundation, the Molossus Fund, and the Saul and Simon Bliss Monboddo Charitable Trust (which has just honored me as its first "Touchstone of the Coming Century" award). What if Broadway is still largely in the vise-grip of ageing Typhon white-boys like Henry Fritz Pettibone and Shaula Silverman, adalpated blowhards from the decline of vaudeville; what if, indeed? After *Snaring Jackdaws*, my radically upbeat, uptempo historical docu-dramedy through, and of, our people's drumming and mummery from the Jim Crow era up to and including my own apprentice days in the racist Abednego of Chenango State, they could not deny me. They could not deny me. My other truly sizzling show, *Dead Souls of Black Folk,* will appear next Spring in all the classy european festivals. It trails a mythical grandfather of W. E. B. Dubois as he travels by stage-coach buying up the dead souls of black folks who have swallowed the official Lincoln line (I mean, there's a reason they called him "The Gorilla"), the whole emancipation swindle; and thus lost their last true possessions, their souls to the hate-filled ghouls in the Freedman's Bureau (in my version a precursor of the Zionist contagion that only by a hair's-breadth spared historic Uganda as the phony, new Jewish homeland). In the Del Mar try-out Frich called it "Black gold—Pure Ebony Gogol" and raved; that boy, he's in my pocket. There is music, dance—only none of that chitlin' circuit gospel and Aunt Jemimah jive, shit no. DuBois *granpere* is a very contemporary and fabulous beebop prototype; a little Mingus, a little Coltrane, and a lot of me. He has visions of Islamic mythopoesis, all arabesque and elegant tracery from the stories portrayed by the Persian miniaturists. He discovers a Sufi master at Confederate Crossroads, Kentucky (name changed to Napahooma Corners after the war) who reveals to him the next three-hundred and fifty years of African-American history, in which I appear in a small but telling and flat-out fabulous cameo as the latest incarnation of the boy-genius Black Isis who spreads terror and confusion at a meeting of the Stage and Screen Directors Guild, which has once more denied me their highest honor, the Jerome P. Jerome "Faster, Louder, Funnier" Award at the annual banquet at the Odeon in downtown Chenango. As Black Isis I release a cacophonous murder of jackdaws who flap about cawing, pecking and crapping in the Guild punchbowl. Dubois changes his name to Shabazz Dubois, and vows to make damn sure all the things Black Isis has revealed do in fact come to pass. Just because the truth is true doesn't mean the keepers of the flame can fall asleep at the wheel. History is like an old sedan, a Nash Rambler for instance, that needs a swift kick in the side-parts every now and again.

~

Still I confess to being fond of history because, the way I see it, history is on my side. Of course this has not always been the case for people like me. My ancestors struggled and struggled and just barely got by. A lot of them never made it, but that's the breaks. I see history as a row of cut-outs, photos of the recent past as it flows back ineluctably to the not-so recent; what used to be called the **pre**-historic, an ever renewable resource. I see each of these cut-outs as an instance of moral and political instruction. Furthermore, there are reasons why certain things come to pass, come into being, and why other things do not. All this I have learned from a close study of Malcolm, C. L. R. James and my true master and only mentor, Riley Dogg Potts, now emeritus at Chenango State where he is a perennial prickle in the hide of the Ice-people in the administration. But more of him later; I want to discourse upon the nature of history, and why we ought to reject the view that it is senseless, random or merely at odds with itself. Because history is not senseless, random or merely at odds with itself. For there is always a cunning purpose buried deep in the wreckage of the most appalling of it. Borrowing the language of the oppressor, this is the perennial nigger in the woodpile. This cunning purpose I would call the Principle of Riley's Revenge, or Legba's Leg-Up Factor; it is the notion, basically, that what goes around comes around and that even the most grievous of historical calamities, like the institution of slavery, the AIDS crisis (I'm not so sure about the so-called "Holocaust," but let's not get into that right now) do in fact serve some higher purpose, only that higher purpose only begins to emerge later on down the line. That is what makes sense of the Bible, for instance: a curious displacement of meaningfulness till later on down the line. My friend Super would dispute all this, and takes a more nihilistic position in general. I suppose that's why he's stuck at WPOO as a mid-level flack for a lot of smug, phony-liberal whitefolk while I am doing my fabulous things being the toast of the town whatever I do.

~

But I digress. For what I really did say to that Darkwood bitch and all those other bitches (in their sable coats) was that I was the only one capable of saving the Rep. "Mad Daddy" Moonbrick was a lunatic—he demanded his staff fill out a separate requisition slip each time they needed an eraser or an envelope; also he was caught making obscene and threatening phone calls (to his Platinum Circle Angels) after the disastrous opening of the road-show of MISERABLE BLOB. As for his successor, Board, well let's just say he has remained all his life a grown-up mall-rat; the kind of egregious white boy who thinks he's cool by copping attitude from Snoop Doggy Dog and Tupac Shakur. A perfectly terrible director, as everyone knows, and not much better as a fund-raiser. I mean you haven't lived until you have heard Mister Van Renssalaer Board provide, with a straight face, the Marxist explanation of why the Rep simply must produce *A Funny Thing Happened to Danny and the Deep Blue Tea Antipathy*. Still, I always got along with the man, on a personal level, you understand. I mean he never did anything to get in my way, which is more than I can say for most egregious white-boys. And he'd always back me up at the board meetings of the Theatre Guild; that time I went ballistic after they put a photo of *Phantom Lease* on the cover of their cheesy rag, and not one from *Black Im Black* which had just scored big in the Apollo workshop at Domely. Told off that mothafucker that runs the place, Malcolm Liverwurst, a clueless hack from beyond the outer perimeter of the Yellow Pages, along with James Earl, that Tom.

At that time I never felt I needed a base. Work on my big musicals. Theaters, black and white, all of them courted me. Trouble with all the African-American theatres (all both of them, I mean) is that black folks don't know how to take orders, and that's a fact. Most of 'em just as clueless and talentless as all those whiny white women I'll have to clear out of here—if I do take the job. A whole shit-load of unhip breeders and low-grade fishes. But my tactic with all mad-dog proto-fascist racist scum is always the same: to undercut and subvert the poison of the hegemonic world-view expressed implicitly in whatever they say or do, by simply accepting their terms of discussion, their definitions meant to neutralize my historically-justifiable killing rage, all unknowing. Then I wheel these about, set my sights so that my fabulous fire-power may achieve the widest sweep and rake them all where they stand, crawl or hide in their ditches, for best effect. My *Othello* is set in Haiti, during the time of Toussaint and Dessalines; Desdemona is the French Commander's daughter, a deranged white slut, of course. Presiding over the whole were a pantheon of the *Loas*, dark African spirits of retribution. Along with Black Isis, played with delicious grace and sexiness by Jewel Bontemps, formerly a student of mine at Chenango State where I taught briefly before I had become my full, fabulous self.

The key is accessibility, and maintaining a tight grip on the means of production. And keeping all eyes focussed on the color line; because that is what Dubois for all his brilliance did not get and what Riley did (and still does, even if he's slowed down a little). Because if all eyes are not fixed on the color line the whole enterprise might well founder. If the Grinding Spoon brags a little too much for some (white) folks pleasure, as the Dogon saying goes, that's because he is only looking forward to grinding down the Palm Nut.

Riley taught me a whole lot more than all the names and proper uses of all the several score of Dogon masks; he taught me how to read the text of the world, especially as it is constructed on the other side of the color line. In his early days in fact he corresponded with Dubois, and later visited the old revolutionary in Accra just a little before he died. Riley admired Dubois but found him lacking a sound ideological basis for his diverse and praiseworthy sociological studies. Shortly after this time he travelled to Tubingen, in Germany, to work on philosophy and historiography; it was there he heard Cermak lecture in the *bier*-halls, along with his brilliant young American secretary, T. N. Thorny, Jr. who was doing work on the General Theory of Non-Aryan Blood-Race and Hydraulicism (Wittfogel). Later, Riley and Thorny discussed many taboo topics during those long summer nights in the cafes of Perdita: the ideas of Cermak, Heidegger and DeMaistre; how no culture can remake itself through such idle things as written laws and constitutions. That only the deep, rich black earth of race pride and blood pride can nurture and support a truly fabulous human crop. This Thorny dude was a strange, dark-eyed figure who wore a fez, in the local custom, and smoked *kef*. Friends called him "Crowe." He seemed to know everything and everyone, had corresponded even with Dubois and reviewed all three volumes of *The Black Flame* trilogy for the *Student Spear*, an international journal dealing with occult and spiritualist subjects, paid for by a certain Flemish cousin of Voljak, the late strongman of Perfidia. I think Thorny was the only white man Riley ever trusted. Years later after the Ice-people had tried to ice him by taking away his department (being tenured he remained a full professor, but alone, all by himself, twisting in the wind) he often spoke of his admiration for that man, and the integrity he possessed to pursue the life of the mind as an isolato, entirely unsupported by the evil grasp of institutions, institutions public or private. For I think Riley, at heart, loved the role of loose cannon, and would say those really provocative things, those things some (and not I) call hateful partly because all those white boy Deans had taken his department away and partly just because he felt like it. All those white liberals never got tired of proclaiming they believed in freedom of speech on the one hand, and of how much they wanted to do everything in their power to eliminate race prejudice. And he knew, deep down, that none of them cared a wooden nickel about either. This all was just so much expensive talk, talk meant for public consumption on the other side of the color line. Where all those serious-minded, endlessly hopeful coons would swallow anything.

We were here, but we were not of here, he would instruct me in his profound basso. Indeed, when one considers the whole problem like a complex crystal rotated in three-dimensional space one can still say today, We are here, but we are not of here. And if you say, as the heirs of Dubois and his nit-picking epigones, all those Black women (like Celise, Yolande and Norine), playwrights who believe that artsy-fartsy line, that a play actually creates its own audience, its own

190

living context; if you say like them, if you say to me: The struggle has to get more closely defined, more grounded, more local, more damn specific, with reference to stuff actually happening in the here and now, I must reply by drawing a line in the sand. Because it is precisely Dubois' bewildering obsession with facticity that I must take exception to—all those ornery, unlovely epistemological widgets and doodads upon which the tents of the Unreal are constructed. Dubois never understood how simple facts are not so simple, how they simply don't matter. Social constructions do. And that goes for a whole lot of people of color now, the kind that have trouble with my fabulous way of doing things.

Every now and then I go visit Riley in his shadowy garden apartment downtown in Chenango, and we discuss his collection of Dogon masks, and the nature of time and perpetual revolution. Things dear to both of us. I was just an insecure undergraduate hoofer in the college's production of, ah, was it *Snaring Jackdaws's* (not my very hip very cool version, but the white boy one it supplanted, by some cracker lady name of

Matilda Waterhead, an awful piece of the most egregious Gershwinistic cross-cultural misappropriation one could ever imagine)? Riley showed up one day with the whole African Studies department gathered around, him glowering like an immense Power Figure from the innermost regions of the Congo Basin. You, he shouted at me, what are you doing up there, son, making a mockery of your ancestors? And I knew in my heart that he was right, and that moment decided my career in as long as it takes to peel a grape. Only now Riley mostly sits there, thinking. It is me who does the talking.

Because, I say to him, and the undertow of what I say is probably quite different from what I'd actually said to that She-Wolf of hatred, Lydia Yaddo Darkwood because around people like her you have to talk all that safe talk about "community" and "under-represented minorities" and "affirmative action" and such shit even while you know all of it, the whole shebang, boils down to a single, unshakable resolve: to make up for every outrage committed against me and my people going all the way back to the days of Ham and

Hagar. And in this struggle the figure of Black Isis shall be the Presiding Genius of our people as we go forth, arm in arm, to take on the forces of Seti, Setuthu, Set, wherever we encounter them in the Not-for-profit industries of this benighted despotism. What I say pleases my master-mentor I know, even though he mostly doesn't say very much in reply.

And besides something tells me I'd better not count all my jackdaws till they're hatched, and I've heard a lot of frankly negative feedback on the workshop of *Black Im Black;* and, hey, this is no "Springtime for Hitler" whatever else it is. The Caucasian elite, especially the old money crowd that hangs with Senator Button and the Freylingheusens at the Epoch Club imagine that they can defang every threat by use of ironic twist. Everything's just a joke to folks like that. Stoppard and Spudly, and all those little metaphysical plays by Grindleshaft. But as my staunch ally in the editorial pages of the *Torpedo,* Perfect Prentiss has recently proclaimed, irony, which was a rapier-like weapon of intellect and of freedom's relentless sallying forth even as late as the time of Oscar Wilde, has become in our time a mere excuse not to come clean concerning one's deeply held homophobia and racism. One's intractable recidivism. Irony is a hollow mask. Irony is a hollow mask because if you don't know what it is you have to say you shouldn't say it. Simple as that; you shouldn't. Because the only doubleness those of us who truly are, in the fabulous sense, politically correct, will admit is the doubleness of the color line. The doubleness of irony is either double-dealing or double-talk. In either case it will not do.

~

So, I do not know whether I will be coming back to Great Wind after all this blows over. Depends whether I get what I want. All of it. Riley would caution prudence; and with true grotesque bigots like Bildad Rasor still holding forth on Capitol Hill I suppose I should listen, listen closely. But the kind of politics it takes to move whole communities, to move their viewpoints and opinions and very souls, is glacially slow, too slow for *moi*.

Leave all that to the Toms and Oreos who want to impress everyone with how rational they are, how accommodating; who want to come out smelling like roses. I don't care about any of that.

I still think of my gaunt-cheeked grandmother sitting in an old chair on the front porch. Wind is creaking through boughs on the big cottonwoods. I look at the red earth, worked out generations ago. I look at the water rush by, gray-green and greasy summer water of the Flint River as it ruffles on, hurrying to join the Chattahoochee. I think of my father who is not there, Toufic a Lebanese queer operating a carpet business out of the back of a flatbed. I think of the year 1954. I have made my way in the world despite every obstacle the white man has hurled down in my path. I have gone on beyond my ancestors, and my poor half-wit brother, Cass.

All I did, or Riley ever did, was to look those hypocritical white liberals straight in the eye, and take them at their word. And what is the nature of Riley's revenge against the Invisible Nation of the Ice-People for their crimes against him at Chenango State?

I am.

Because no one ever did that, take them exactly for their word, no more, no less.

VI: Van

21 [FROM BEYOND THE GRAVE]:

Quilp. Quilp. Quilp. My fingers feel so roundy and quilth. As if I were taken suddenly away, like the windborn air-bleb or tassel of thornyflower on an invisible curlicue of air, out on the wild prairies of New Baskets. My consciousneth like a shadow on the water of the Old and Lost Rivers of Rome, Palmyra and Domely Heights. Like I were a human cushion, without shape or boundary. For I am without shape or boundary. For I am now a phantom, a brutally untenanted ghost who was once the Artistic Director of one of the most respected regional theatres, Great Wind Repertory; and now I am less than the breezes that gently rock the fruit-laden boughs in the orchards of Sweet Thumb, Athens and Troy. I am a dim and unappeased spirit who shall never cross Lethe because I possess no coin for the Boatman. Who shall mourn for me and raise monuments to my deeds? Who shall mark the earth with my stone and bolt the bronze plaque to the wall in the lobby along with those of our patrons and benefactors? Who will recall my sly wit, my lustrous pony-tail and neatly trimmed Artistic Director's beard, all of the approved cut and style? Who shall remember my deftness at parrying the uncomprehending and irate subscriber at our talk-back sessions, at convincing the skeptical local bigshot that the theatre is an important and vital social practice, at dealing with the suspicious and frequently hostile philistines at the local office of Congressman Harvey P. Smathers, Republican Revolutionary and thirty-one year old self-made millionaire in the thriving V-chip industry north of Old Ham, east of Oswego, at negotiating effectively with the dull and complacent representatives of the Actors Equity Association as they attempt, time after time, to extract blood from stones in contract talks so maddeningly intricate and Byzantine they would hardly seem out of place back in the Sanjak of Perfidia where I used to roam during one strange and fateful summer off from the Groaner School of Drama from which I alone of my class have prospered and achieved something like a modest success in the theatre while my classmates in Direction,

Marketing and Management—Bim "Motor-mouth" Porter, Jessica Furbelow, and that ass, Clarice Novotny—have all faded into various pockets of obscurity as flacks, copywriters at houses of persiflage, and slogged along as mid-level, terminally attenuated perpetual disappointments to the world and, by implication, to themselves as well? Who will remember and cherish my honest and serviceable production of *Snow Boat*, my legendary remounting of *Dromedary at Thirty-third Street*, and the sweet hijinks and simplehearted laughter of my *Corn Ascending*, of which Frich wrote,…laughed so hard the tears wrinkled my playbill? Who?

No one, my bitter heart tells me, not a single living soul under the dreary sixty-watt lightbulb of the moon, moon swaying gently overhead, where my poor head once was. My careless curls, once caressed by teenage lovers at Gridly Prep and Monsanto College, then tugged at—hard—by paramours in the Stage Management Division of Groaner, now ruined and dead. And I unknowable now and forever, attached only to my name that drifts perilously high, high overhead like a child's balloon. The name Board, ancient roundish name of my clan, also a noble plank or piece of timber, human timber only seeking a purpose and fitting use. But now my board is shattered and shivered from stem to stern in a fast flurry of blows I cannot but briefly recall. A flurry of blurs. A blur of blows falling hard upon me in a blur of dire sensation; as disconnected seemingly from what followed as by what preceded so that I do not even know the name of my destroyer.

My murder has a distinctly postmodern edge to it; somehow, this death of mine smacks of an erasure. A cold act of malevolent erasure plotted in full cognizance of likelihoods and the Delta Array of possible consequence. I am proud of my murder as there is also something fateful and Greekish about it, like those old plays by Aeschylus, Sophocles and Mosschops that drove even my most seasoned subscribers to states of dire distraction and wilted anomie. Crushingly profound, crushingly tedious. Something about the grave becomes me, and my slack and slightly wooden ways. Just as no person truly touched me after the death of my sweet Great Aunt Julia, lost, lost forever in a tangle of wild Sumatran water lilies in that horrible boating accident at Dunlop Bay, near the Water Filtration Plant; so now, I am rounded off with an incomplete French curve of a question mark that will be left hanging in everyone's mind. If, indeed, there are any who shall truly mourn me, and not simply make an idle and grotesque parade of an emotion they do not feel.

If a man is not a little feared, someone said, he will not be remembered with much affection. That gnaws at me. For it just now occurs to me that I am trying to grasp what has happened, and understand the full force of it; that I am exploring the borders and boundaries of being dead.

Let us begin by establishing a certain parameter.

For there is, without a doubt a metaphysic of the grave.

This is the first proposition in that metaphysic: That the same order of logic that operates in the world of the living, which is to say, the world of Not-for-Profit theatre, in all its forms and galas and more or less shoddy productions of the less challenging Classics, more or less "hot" warm and clutchy single issue small cast plays and related NAPs and post-play discussions and workshops of varying kind and of course staged readings and cold readings and conferences, round tables, square tables and phone calls, faxes and e-mail. Visits to alien web sites of other orthodox institutional theatres and theatre organizations of every conceivable kind, The Players' Club in Troy craft unions and guilds for the various sorts of theatre-worker whether paid, nonpaid or dues paying. Cabals and conspiracies of those embittered, paranoid and excluded, whether by pure structural necessity, or by conscious design of the gatekeepers in questions, whether on the Board of Directors, The Advisory Board, or on the play-reading committee, the Benefit Committee, or the Theatre Panel of the State Arts Council convened semi-annually behind locked doors in Rome; or by their own mediocrity, lunacy, bad attitude, mendacity, or sheer bone-headed bad timing or other non-specific self-induced folly. The logic of all this, the world of the living and the logic of the world of the grave must be, surely, if we are not to succumb to sheer terror and madness, of the same sort; so that the logic of the living must obtain in the world of the dead just as the logic of the living obtains in the world of the living; so that the logic of the dead likewise obtains in the world of the living just as the logic of the dead does so in the world of the dead. This basic structure must surely be in place, if we are to make any sense of the situation. Surely it must, for otherwise the fierce drama of meaninglessness, *Anangke*, Positive Negation, would be buried in the very stuff of existence causing us to start up, and stop—but way, way beyond the Fear and Pity of Aristotle, bringing us to the door of Terror and Madness, the strange world of what is wholly without meaning.

What matters is what matters, surely. Even beyond the borders of the grave.

I cannot recall anything so strange and disturbing since I spent many hours behind my bathroom mirror, while at Groaner, learning how to use my hands and arms more effectively while engaged in public speaking. It proved extremely difficult for me to acquire the knack, but the example of Professor Swanhope inspired me so much that I doggedly persevered despite my gangly and unruly fore-limbs. At times they seemed in open rebellion against the jurisdiction of gestural decorum and sweet reasonableness itself. At the least emotion I would find myself sawing the air, sawing the air in a fashion always at odds with the text or speech I was reciting. On occasions those near to me physically would actually flinch or draw away as if in sudden horror, so gangly and shaggy were my movements. It seemed that I could only produce a pleasing and harmonious, not to mention pleasingly expressive, body language if I wasted literally none of my diffuse powers of concentration on speaking whatever it was I was speaking. This resulted in a tendency to drone, a life-long tendency it should be noted, which I was only able to amend somewhat by recourse to Pizazz, an over-the-counter nonprescription medicine for which I possess much enthusiasm. Pizazz marked a milestone in my life, and enabled me to address large groups of actors, audience members, not to mention the well-off (prized contributors and donors at their clubs and convention halls). Pizazz enabled me to realize myself as a respected member of the theatre community. I recommend Pizazz to all those who, for no fault of their own, find themselves likely to falter, or to fall into fits. Fall into fits of anguish, anguish and worse. Indeed, I wish there were a medicine such as Pizazz designed to quell my current anguish. Because it is not so much being dead that appalls me; it is that I have no idea where I am. Pieces of my past float about, and remind me of the mirror in the bathroom of my human soul, the mirror that now is shattered, that was once whole and new. That reassuring mirror that doubled as the door to the medicine cabinet of my very being. Now I feel only a curious doubleness, as if when I put my foot down on whatever sheer surface lies below, another image of me is simultaneously placing his foot congruently on the bottom of my sole in a weird, upside-down world. An existential echo of my own, except I am unsure whether he (or I) is the type of the true Van Rensselaer Board or merely his (or my) parody. Similarly, the place where my limbs once joined and fused seems now a mere void. Absence infuses me, and a powerful doubt concerning...well, concerning everything. All I seem able to perceive is what feels like the riffling of a hot, humid night breeze on thin, gauzy curtains of a motel, say, at Paradigm Key along the North New Digits archipelago where I vacationed with dear Peanut Phillips so many years ago, just after the failure of my thesis production at Groaner, *King Yam*. That, and what sounds like a telephone ringing, ringing in the distance. Distant, but not too far.

If I could only make my way to that telephone, and answer it, I know I would hear a voice as sweet as heaven's water flowing over me in pretty twists and knots, lots of knots like those women of color are fond of tying in their hair. And this voice would be the voice of the moon, Luna, and it would say something extraordinarily sweet and simple to me. Dear one, it would say, don't be afraid. Everything you fought for and struggled on behalf of, everything...even all those terrible new American plays with their sentimental mimble-mamble, vulgar chest-thumping, and sheer theatrical stupor; all these were worth the aggravation, even horrible pieces of misbegotten dreck like *Bonerlaw's Fistula* and *Greaser Paydirt* and *Freaky Pussy* and that truly awful slacker-musicale *Beige: A Utah Mellowdrama;* all these foul abortions, which you dutifully commissioned or encouraged by hint or suggestion, by a wink or a subtle prod; all these you carefully nurtured, Van, in the hope that something wonderful might come of it...somehow, against all doubt and rational calculation...somehow, yes. Even that ghastly...*Fish-head*...; quilp, quilp, quilp. No, no. And the absolute nadir, also of Chris Name's doing, *Q's Q.* Unspeakable. But no, no, your faith inspired not only your entire staff, from bumbling, neo-fascist Connie, to that jaded, bitter, over-the-hill jambon John Dough$_2$, even sour little Pooh who could have been pretty if she'd've lost some of the black leather and chains, and hadn't pierced every visible flap and fold of her pale, oh so pale exterior integumenta; all, despite their failings and tiresome mediocrity, regarded you as a searchlight, as an inspiriting beacon, a flare of inspiration and Thespian resolve. This voice would tell me where I truly am, not in the actual hell of holes and flame, but in a sort of half-way house for those whose proper place in classical times would surely have been Limbo: An inclosed private community, or mall, where the feckless, unhoused spirits might wander, in their weeds and shrouds, conversing in low tones about funding projections, subscriber bases, and the importance of theatre to the American soul, and as a nursery for the film industry. Or: the voice would merely assure me that none of this matters anymore because I, Van Rensselaer Board, have arrived at a new and higher spiritual plateau where the busyness and pettifoggery of the daily shall seem, at last, what it truly is: a harmless passel of toots, and eructation. *Nada mas.*

Although, perhaps I am mistaken in this regard.

Perhaps the moon would tell me other, stranger things. Narratives of gleaming strangeness. Maybe the moon would tell me what can be described can happen too, and what is excluded by the law of causality cannot be described. Maybe it would tell me the World is independent of my will; that Ethics cannot be expressed, that Ethics is transcendental (Ethics and Aesthetics are one). Maybe, maybe even it would suggest that the Kantian problem of the right and left hand which cannot be made to cover one another already exists in the plane, and even in one-dimensional space; where two congruent figures **a** and **b** cannot be made to cover one another without

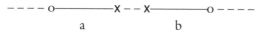

         a   b

moving them out of this space. That the right and left hand are in fact completely congruent. And that the fact that they cannot be made to cover one another has nothing to do with it; because a right-hand glove could be put on a left hand if it could be turned round in four-dimensional space. And furthermore, what if the moon is correct and I am merely a right-handed glove that has been turned round in four-dimensional space so as to be able to fit a left hand?

I must not allow myself to think such thoughts.

Such thoughts are unthinkable.

Such thoughts are downright evilish, and do not comport with my picture of the world. My picture of the world is a meaningful picture with God, there is a god in it, at the top. A pleasant, hominid god (like me but older). Even though I was never much of a practicing Christian since my undergraduate days when I read Nietzsche and *Totem and Taboo*...which reminds me of my workshop of the musical theatre revue based on an adaptation of that august tome by the noted Ogilvy P. Isinglass of Pomfret College in the smokey forest region of regal New Delbert...one of my finest apprentice works, and which caught the attention of the young and up-and-coming Frich who was covering the summer stock and thoroughbred racing season upstate for the New Burdock *Miscellany*, a lank and languid publication.

No, no, no.

22 [CORN ASCENDING]:

For now my reverie takes wing and soars back to my salad days, when I was cutting my teeth on the classics, NAPs too numerous to enumerate, and the occasional urgently topical and always newsworthy docu-dramedy. Each passing day flew past, like a thing that flits. My friends Gary and Zach and Yony and Iat, at the Cremation Chamber Theatre, outdid themselves in contriving cutting-edge drama, though never with a scornful disregard for the audience and the moral habits of the community at large, a perennial weakness of the traditional, and terminally elitist, avant-garde.

One thing no one could, in good conscience, call me is an elitist.

I am not an elitist.

Who can forget *Corn Ascending*, probably the best thing I ever did, about the true story of Lars Underruud, an epic and out-sized outdoorsman and successful agriculturalist who dispatched his wife Anya and their seven children, one by one, in his roaring John Deere hay-bailing machine under direct order from a stern and unflinching God on high; a God whose word meant more than anything to that humble and devout soul, whose alcoholic and frequently demented parents abused him psychologically, sexually, and verbally over a long and gloomy adolescence (abused, co-incidentally, under a similar edict from a similar hard and profoundly covered God).

Oh, and the rousing quadrille of the Corn Girls and Corn Boys and the Tasselled Ones and Plug the Happy Woodsman and the Cheerful chanticleer Weathervane whose cockle-cockle clock-clock cocklelorum reminds all who pay heed that bad weather and the evils of chronic depression are as soap bubbles in the wind and ought not be dwelled upon; the heroine, Martha Hingewafer, who nurtures poor Lars at the Home for Incurables in Radiator Heights where he has been confined for his crimes and subjected to mental torture and repeated psychological testing by the malicious Doctor Merle Fainsod, a notorious professional necrophile and part-time private sadist from Deep Pockets, upstate in the

Minerva Hills of New Dinah, a remote and arid region noted for a long history of notorious necrophiles and private sadists; the sign from God on high that his almighty intention is, in Lars' poor case, redemptive and salvatory: The apocalyptic appearance, high overhead the prosperous fields of New Domino and North Delightful, of an enormous wheel of solid cheddar cheese, surrounded by an aureate nimbus emblazoned with the tetragrammaton, in dazzling scarlet and black. And who can ever forget the soaring optimism of the final hoe-down roundelay "Hope, hope is the soul's melodious soap!," an optimism that has proved irresistible wherever the show has been mounted, and all during its six month run at the Majestic in Athens.

True, I never made much money off the thing. My agent at the time, Reynolds Class (also the agent of Marshal "Mad Daddy" Moonbrick, it should be noted) proved an unscrupulous fraud, and totally botched the contract so that the sleazy hacks I'd hired to flesh out my ideas, and deal with dialogue, character and continuity, came away with the lion's share. I am of course referring to Duke "Pepe" Rococo and Brett Whipp, no talent goons whose graceless collaborations include such obvious turkeys as *Fat Boys in Grass Skirts* and *A Trick Rat,* both complete duds at Gogol Rep seven or eight years ago. But there is no justice in the world, and if I had done the things I've done only for money I'd have been out of my mind, or like one afflicted (like poor Lars in the sequel I could never get backing for, *Amazing Maize)* with a lesion on the occipital lobe leaving him with the recurring, obsessional delusion of being gagged, bound and tossed for long periods of time in a Simmons Pot. A man with a ruined sense of judgment, and a highly restricted credit line.

In those days the future lay before me like an immense and well-manicured lawn, green and roundy. The future seemed arranged for my personal comfort and amusement, with no threat or care anywhere to be seen. Like that time—well-earned down-time—with sweet Peanut, drifting in pointless sunlight in our battered, rental dingy of pink and ivy-green spruce, floating at the exact center of Mascardi Lake, lost in the mangroves

and Spanish moss and nullity of New South Digits, unbelievably happy.

23 [A FEW DOUBTS CREEP CREEPILY IN]:

I shall, however, pass over in silence those few, depraved months back in the Sanjak with only the remark that I have become convinced—picking up on a tip that Constantine has darkly suggested—that, unknowingly I was somehow, somewhere during that dismal sojourn, the victim of the Perfidian *mal'uocchiu*. The Evil Eye. I cannot substantiate this charge, I know; but I know it to be true, I just know it. In any event, the slow, steady consolidation of my early career culminated, I guess you could say, with a brief stint as assistant to Giles Mulebrae at the renowned Royal Academy of Grimly; Associate to Gerard Shannonball out west in sunny Del Marvela, a place of pink and tawny stucco'd profusion, an endless Springtime of audiences so dumbed-down by solar glare and television they hardly knew they were supposed to applaud at the end of a play; but, obversely, would balk at nothing, even plays as hopeless as Daphne Blue's *I Was a Human Delivery Cylinder* and that unlikely hit from New Delibes (or was it New Deli?), *The Riddle of the Revolving Door*. Then "Mad Daddy" Moonbrick had to be removed, croaking and mooing, to the Sacculate Chamber at Saint Nebulosity's, a strange old pile out by the moors near Lake Immanity, and Jake was brought in as interim AD. Jake's own career was already stratospheric so he had no intention of hanging out here long, in the tri-state area, a proverbial frog-hollow. I was approached by a cousin of the Cabot Lodges named Anne Raife Wrigley, a chthonic engineer widely known for her research on Recoatibility and Recognition Feedback in Smith-Gravely Sequences, also a prominent member of the Search Committee. I liked her, she liked me. When we discussed the matter she tossed her bleached shock of hair in a suggestive way. Only thirty, she recognized the importance of bringing new blood into the institutional torso and taking action to do something about the blue-hairification of the subscription audience, a feedback loop in dire need of major recoating. In a tinkle of a Smith-Gravely tingle I had the whole joint in the palm of my big hand,

and was being honored at an elegant luncheon at the Pierre in Clotilde Park, a swank suburb of Rome.

In the first, airy days everything felt easy; we programmed whatever was a hit in New York or a buzz in Chenango. We commissioned the Obvious to write the Obvious, directed usually with obvious competence by obvious choices, and played by actors of obvious talent. Lights, obvious; scenic design, also obvious. For the rest we relied on the wisdom of Elvis in Marketing, one of only two white shirts in the building, a man with a suspicious personal life and an unerring instinct for how risky one could go in programming. And that "how risky" was not very.

But, slowly at first and then more rapidly, doubts began to creepily arise in the rear-view mirror of my partially submerged consciousneth. These doubts moved with shadowy stealth, and eluded easy definition. A vague sense of unease permeated the closed torus-ellipsoid of the Rep's HVAC system. For a time I suspected we had been visited by Sick Building Syndrome (SBS), and in a midnight fury I tore out the ceiling of the Conference Room C-3, convinced I would find there a suspicious, toxic mold. In the morning I felt abashed, and was obliged to offer apologies to the Building Manager, Frank Nolan, a fellow lapsed Rotor-Rosicrucian, and a fairly accomplished accordionist at office bashes. But slowly it dawned on me that my doubts were not metaphysical ids and nonentities, but actual beings, people, the people I had hired, supported, nurtured, loved and bonded with in our rehearsal halls, in perilous talkback sessions, and at our summer retreats in the Marlowe House just at the forest line on splendid Mount Slagtop perched high above Deluge Bay, at our softball games, and at Zip C's Grill, a hot jive joint favored by out-of-town actors and the black leather set. Nine Inch Nail wannabes like Pooh, and Chainsaw, our cross-eyed TD from Mahwah. I began to realize with horrible clarity how difficult it is to be surrounded by lazy, incompetent, lying, dishonest fools, dolts, semiliterate boors and sociopaths; I realized that nothing, literally nothing, would get done without my watchful supervision. Accordingly, I discretely arranged for the installation of a system of hidden mirrors and Remote Video Viewing stations (or RVVs) recommended by Anne, and designed by a colleague of hers at IBEX, a rising security services conglomerate.

I discovered what a very great pleasure it is to monitor one's employees.

I discovered much about their meaningless tics and habits, and how much the same these are when observed as when not observed—as long as the employee is not aware of being observed. Only, one never really finds out what one needs to know about them, the little people, flickering like they were phantoms in a virtual reality game, or like the lost ones wriggling forever in their Challenge Box in that play by Old Malone. Because one can never really completely penetrate the complex world of human motivation, and as Aristotle (I think it was Aristotle) and Swanhope have argued: Motivation is the key to understanding human behavior. One might even go so far as to say the behavior only shows up after the fact, the fact of motivation, to justify its existence. Much the same may well be true of life in general: Of love affairs, crimes, extraordinary achievements of planning, execution and even the work of monitoring itself; for the facts must arrange themselves neatly in a line and not randomly be tossed, as a handful of jellybeans are tossed—yes, in a line, whether straight, curved or diabolically wiggly, for a demonstrable purpose to be inferable. This is sometimes not so easy to achieve.

All this digression stands as proof positive that an observant eye is, indeed, capable of rendering in absolute entirety the visible world and all it contains; and of recreating it, redescribing this fluid phantom every day, anew. As I considered the deeper implications of sheer visibility I began to understand the dark, hidden wisdom of my illustrious predecessors in the Artistic Director pantheon—giants like Tyrone, Joe and Zelda; Earle and Sven. Billy and Nigel; even "Mad Daddy" himself before the trip to Sumatra, where he picked up that unlucky infection (Zeisler's Morbula), the same that sent him into his legendary savage, senseless rages. For all these visionary power-brokers understood the dark necessity for art to be a mechanism, through the vortices of the visible and its orbicular extensions, of social conditioning. They also understood, by application of similar rule, the wisdom of the old aphorism—it is not enough for your children to succeed; they must also fail.

And, thus, I felt a surge of powerful emotion as I observed small, mediocre Pooh (in my convex lens) nibbling on nothing, as she devoured one after another, unreadable volumes of Critical Theory and stacks of plays so misbegotten they seem crimes against the arboreal continuum itself. Or crazed Connie, lost in the vegetative nightmare of Eastern Europe, a nightmare from which he would never awake and realize he was not entitled to storm unannounced into a Season Planning Meeting demanding to know how to spell "potatoe." As for John Dough$_2$—pleez; or our Business Manager, Ronald R. Rector, whose total lack of fiscal imagination has dogged me daily, night and day, the last few years; and whose every word, whether spoken or by written memo, seems to contain an implicit recrimination and always, always, especially after the failure of our Christmas pageant, *Santas from Hell,* my highly original reworking of *A Christmas Carol* (with some powerful new material from the Holocaust {juicy tidbits from camp life at Sobibor and Mauthasen} tastefully layered in), I sense his cold reptile stare on the back of my neck, causing the hairs that live there (that used to live there) to prickle, prickle, prickle. Even dead hair responds to the uncanny.

But the worst of all, the image that has haunted me to the grave and beyond, the image that has annealed my torn and broken limbs; annealed them in pure horror and abstraction is that of that demented, talentless fool Chris Name raving, raving at the conclusion of his staged reading of *Q's Q* (why oh why did I ever listen to Pooh, that mousy manipulator of man alone, as well as maniples of men?); standing before me like a golem, like a reanimated corpse, speaking a language so intensely alien none who heard him could not but feel his or her flesh crawl; speaking the gibberish of an ancient curse or cantrip, a cold puff of such pure malevolence it silenced everyone in the room, even those orgiasts who had begun smashing tables and chairs with their bloody fists, and beating on the windows with enraged shoe-leather.

Was it! Could it have been? Him!

Quilp. Quilp. Quilp. My fingers feel even more roundy and quilth than before. Perhaps as the souls of my torn limbs drift farther and farther apart, all that shall be left of me, my essence, shall be a thimbleful of Van Rensselaerite, a soft white talc which, when wettened and allowed to dry into shapeless lumps, may be worked upon a wheel or lathe, with sharp tools for best effect, and shaped into pleasing shapes. Van Board, van quished.

But now the candle brightens briefly (candle! What candle?) and those last few moments are arranging themselves into sense, like the checkerboard tiles in the Mens at the Green Room. I see it now: The Board Meeting in conference room C3. Ronald R. Rector has just concluded a fiscal report that seems characteristically downbeat. Elvis will not look me in the eye, and this after the trouble I took to procure for him a supply of Enhanced Pizazz, the prescription version with double the voltage of the ordinary. Someone asks me an impertinent question, a question of the sort that deserves no reply, a question that constitutes a snide and aggressive assertion rather than instance of ordinary human curiosity. My last allies on the Board, Anne Wrigley and John Gregg Toledo, both bigwigs at IBEX, look pale and confused. Not Lydia, no. Lydia looks ferocious in her exquisite sable coat which she has coldly declined to remove, citing the inordinate chill of our HVAC (at times I still suspect the Rep to be an undetected victim of SBS); nor do any of the other assembled skirts offer to remove their sable, their fox, their mink, their vicuna; nor, in fact, do any of the assembled suits loosen their neckties, or adjust any portion of their attire in a way that might suggest informality or a casual get-together of amicable parties. For one last time I look at the painting on the wall, a disturbingly iridescent gouache of *Anak Krakatau,* a whitish tuft curling sweetly up from the summit, only a little before the big blow; painted by one of my old patroon great-great uncles, Diemen Van Rensselaer. The tropical scene always reminds me, oddly, of times with Peanut. Then the shouting starts up, and I see Puella and Connie, even, yelling at me with clenched fists; they have discovered (How? How!) my system Remote Viewing Stations (RVVs). Has Chainsaw too betrayed me? Pooh is shrieking in her most shrill Postmodernist whine about what she derisively calls "The Van-Opticon of Van Rensselaer Board." Now I hear other voices, deep hate-filled ones and light, tinkling hate-filled ones, all full of doubt, outrage and hostility. Lydia's fearful visage, horribly swollen with passionate intensity approaches, as if a mighty, pink, roast ham on wheels. Is the room darkening around me, or am I simply going mad? I answer "yes" to all their nasty questions, many of them as pointless and riddling as a curse from *Q's Q. Q's Q?* Lydia roars, roars like a raging boar, surely you cannot be dreaming of mounting that atrocity in your upcoming season? Of course, of course, nothing could be further from my intention, but in my mounting confusion, and besieged on all sides as I am, I can make no sound but a crrk. Even dearest Anne and John Gregg Toledo, my loyal

IBEXs, glare at me with hissy-fit coldness. Crrk, I say and crrk again. What did you say, Lydia roars. What do you mean to say? Answer our question, someone in the back shouts. But now the whole room is seething with rage and rancor. Rage ripples through the fluid air causing it to bend light and sound as water does. No one listens to my protestations. Now they are shouting at each other, and a hat flies off a head like a flying spaceship as these were imagined in the time before digital imaging, but after the death of God. Objects on the table—pencils, pens, paper clips, pads of paper, binder clips and no.1 ideal clamps and other small metallic items begin an insane St Vitus dance as insensibly I find myself backed up to the wall at the long end of the room. But then I see something I truly cannot believe: It is Chris (Is it Chris?), that imbecile, approaching strange and slow, on huge stony feet, arms outstretched Frankenstein fashion. His eyes glare greeny-bright and luminous; his eyes are mad. The last few things I recall: *Santas from Hell,* screamed as a cantrip; an odd sense of myself as an odd hunk of some unlicked transuranic metal sizzling in a glove box while metallic fingers examine me (rotating the stuff of me in four-dimensional space), my event-horizon approaching from all sides as at the speed of light; and as I fade I see fur, and hear a terrible cracking noise—it is my own arm being ripped out of its socket.

VII: Luna

25 [A REPRESENTATION OF THE CRESCENT MOON AS AN ORNAMENTAL LEMON]:

Moon. Maan. Mankind, indeed. The Man in the. Hoo, hoo, (w)hoo. Who sees all things. (W)hoo has no stake in what (s)he sees, all this mutability; for during the entire course of it, from Alpha to Omega, all in the blink of a moonish eye, I, Luna, (w)hoo cannot turn away, must view, forever, the catastrophe you have occasioned, established, perpetuated and celebrate daily in all you (hoo) think (ha) and do (hoo). So now I (eye) tilt in the solar wind, as an apparent profile (hoo) on file, for all to view; for all to view and so misconstrue as some one (hoo) of you (hoo); and this from the time of Sumer and Assyria, and this from the chime of China when the oldest now we—meaning you (hoo)—know was new, and thus all notions of what.

So what at first quarter of Luna is a profile of a human face (w)hoo, or just before, is (w)hoo I am; and, let us say, I (Eye) see out of the corner of a crinkled eye. A merest corner, say. For I cannot turn away, and so must assay the same repetition of folly over and over and over and over till over and over is over and no more than a buzz, a buzz buried in another over and over and this one also is buried in a buzz, and so on till time itself, layer upon layer has built a house of all this, all misprision and misrule.

~

And this is what I see: Far, far away in the Sanjak of Perfidia, a man with a fez rides on a yellow butterfly *(Danaides Bigarrees)* of a bicycle, wobbily weaving all the way from Tamar to Quilq, with the "q" turned accidentally about to become a "p". This man is "Mad" Antony Thornsrule, a radical rotarian and subversive bible salesman, apparently on missionary duty (w)here from the Church of the Re-Animated Samaritan, in far away New Brillo; alone of all of you (hoo) this man I know and recognize.

In every generation, over the ninety thousand

or so I have observed since you have become recognizably (w)hoo you are or human, or fallen into that condition, there have been a few among you of great character and worth; yet nearly all of these have been murdered or corrupted at an early age. Only the tribe of Thorn-devil has escaped detection; only the Thorn-devils have not debased themselves, but have harried everywhere they go the greatest nation of mankind, the FOOLS. And this Thornsrule is deceiving the Re-Animated Samaritans by circulating copies of their sacred Book of Hohokus, filled with pornographic representations of the church fathers, representations of strange and disturbing passion, passion far beyond the orbit of the connubial. Passion with fezzes and screens, whips and rope ladders, musky oils and dimly glowing candela-dada-labra; passion swirling like the finest silk of Gondujar in air heavy with frankincense and myriad option. Thus, rioting and outrage is sure to break out wherever his bicycle has wobbled, followed everywhere by cries of "Jihad" and "Death to Homer P. Granville-Prescott"—the current Samaritan Patriarch—as the gulled Perfidians hurl brickbats at the American consulate in fern-summery Quilq, and break their blackened teeth on their own schistous, creosote-drenched thresholds of Creto-Mycenaean antiquity. And this thorn will evade detection; nay, he will not only escape detection he will join the crowd before the American Embassy in Tamar, chanting cantrips from *Monkey Writing From the Time of Pyramids,* calling out for the death of himself, "Mad" Anthony Thornsrule, his fist shaking in perfect synchronization with two-hundred thousand others along the Avenue of the Twentieth of May, the entire vast openness of the Silver Square of the Nine Thousand Bostangi, a carpet of uplifted faces, all cleft by a single, shadowy hatred.

And he will do these things for reasons which are occult and not easily scannable; because the Thorny obeys the nasty rule and destiny of his Thorndaddy before him, and earlier and thornier Thorndaddies all the way back to the rustic dunes of Western Africa, on the beach at Namibia where the first genius of all the thorns—the primal ur-Thorndaddy—of all the thorns hewed and hacked at a branch of adolescent ironwood, willfully and with malice, to fashion a tool devised solely for the making of counterfeit footprints, footprints faked for the express purpose of deceiving a future archeologist, one Professor Augustus M. Square-Johnly, whose paper on the early hominid "Sandalwood Man" proved the sensational apex of intellectual fashion at Molossus during the same slow, lank season that witnessed Post-Van Great Wind Repertory slide nose first into the deep bog of Chapter Eleven with little more than an unpleasant gassy burp or two.

For even Jake "Burning Spear" Hall could not hide the fearful botch.

And thus all things proceed in the orbit Mutability has arranged for them; each in the private delirium most appropriate, like a hermit crab, or the maleficent Higgins borer-wasp, and all of the truly demonic souls Saint Augustine observed walking in perfect circles, and so walking and so walking, incognizant. For in truth mainly what I observe of the mere and mostly human is the walking of perfect circles, circles of perfectly clueless and meaningless ordinaria. Indeed, circles of such closed-off and sealed spiritual perfection they give those of us of a roughly spherical dimension, and the habit of following an imperfectly elliptical orbit, much to think about, and envy. For while I am round and big, I am covered with bumpy spots and am far from perfect in any wise.

And yet for all my imperfections I am drawn towards the earth, as I am to all that is ornamental. Like the fabric of everlasting night that so sparkles with little points of lights, points of dazzle and brilliants, sparks and brilliants of every hue, that I call it the "Blackdress"; alas, my stiff neck prevents me from ever swinging about, so that I must for all time take in whatever measure of the majesty of the visible I can manage, as it were, over my shoulder. You, dwellers on Terra, my mother and guardian, with her perpetually changing skies, and seas of such azure loveliness that I almost wish I could submerge my being in hers and become, like you, just so much dust come to life (whatever that is!) for a moment or two, lustful, murderous, incurious and vague; so that I might pour her fragrant waters over the hard and tortured clastic flows and fields and impact craters of my dusty and unchanging moonly resolvancy, like a huge lemon (what's a lemon?) in the silvery lustrousness of my ball of borrowed light.

26 [APPROACHING FULL]:

And yet North America scrolls around the globe under the brightly gleaming terminator that divides night from day; once more I must observe Christopher Name whose wolfish inner clockworkery is encased in the usual plebeian palaver. Words! Words! Aren't you ever tired of their immarcesible tyranny? How much more of this witless brouhaha? This peirastic vetanda? And it is no better elsewhere, for as I glide slitheringly and silently, like the Great Rufous Hedge-Owl, far above the granite overbite of the northeast, I witness the natural antitheatrical one might entitle *The Republic of Gloom, or Fat People in the Tee-shirts—A New (Hoo) England Tryptych:* Part One, Incinerating Witches; Two, Alcoholism; Three, the Art of the Unkempt Beard. But there is no time to enjoy this brief diversion before I am high overhead the entire tri-state area.

Below me, ghastly, lies the whole, swollen breadbelly of New Baskets, with its sole legitimate theatre, raving Peanut Phillips' Theatre of the Pre-Existing Condition where Rinehart Man-liblow's *Overproduction of Zuchini* has just opened to wonderful reviews. This awful play intrigues me because it concerns a young man who is driven out of his mind by the Moon, and is so deluded that he dreams he has discovered a way of growing zucchini from common vermiculite; Vernal Hodge is his name, and he is in love with a strange but exotically beautiful exchange student from Tamar (the one back in the Sanjak, not the one in New Delbert where the Kaiser-Fraser Museum is perched a mile up on a spike of malachite overlooking the fantastic gorges of the Talbot River). Anna Kion-Khoth is her name, and she possesses Cuman blood (blood of the Petchenegs! Wild, swearing, moon-worshipping blood!); you can guess the rest.

And on and on, all the usual sardoodledum.

But let me move on, as heavenly bodies are wont to; we who are incapable of occupying a point of rest, or inhabiting the reflex of time's percolation in so-called perfect repose; for now I behold Chris, poor deluded Chris. Strapped dynamite enchrysalises him as a moonbug of unbelievable fatuousness. Such as he, the perennially promising playwrights of the tri-state area are as the silly, tufted shuttlecock, forever being batted back and forth from developmental program to developmental program; from Molossus to Groaner, from Gogol Rep to Great Wind Repertory and beyond; a kind of hardy and resistant spore that shall release its theatrical effluvium wherever it fall, whether within the rank, subtropical humidorium of New South Digits and the gulf, where I smile down poisonously upon mankind and all his works, for all the world like an aggregation of Hyacinth Beans, or far, far, far out upon the cold Arctic granites and schists of windswept New Bellows, where only as an acidulous, ascetic lichen—most lowly form of what you call life—can this life subsist, much less flourish, within the traditional worm-fences and upon the glacial till that litters the place in senseless disarray. For there are things in life not dreamt of by Arthur Fitz-Hugh Royale, Ph.D., in his *Fundamentals of Dramatic Composition;* nor in those of Stankus, Swanhope, or Glory; not even in the magisterial works of Wuvorin and that other chap whose name boasts so many unaccustomed consonants all arranged spikily, hedgehog fashion, as if to ward off some fierce invader from Central Asia, some Uuc or Son of Uuc, hot with the smell of blood, screeching a curse as though summoning demons from the foul regions of the Bauls on Mount Tabun Bagdo, a place remote to most of you but not to me. All things Terran I measure with the same lunatic yard stick, that of my long indifference. Chris knows the demons that sizzle within the Sweet Thumb Reactor's core are more deadly (to some) than all the Resonators and Phantom Sollickers of the Qats, but what can he do? He has been driven mad by ambition, an ambition to accomplish that which lies beyond both his talent and culture. Moannu-moannu waits for him patiently, slowly sharpening his silvery shredding tool at his lake resort on velvety Lake Mascardi; yet Chris in his innocence is doubly damned because he does not even know if he did, or did not, rip poor Van limb from limb; does not know if, in truth, he did not transform at that terrible puncture-wound of Time, crisis-time, and change into something lupine, evilish and vile. A creature the Divine Ones did not intend when they took off on that rare holiday to sunny Christmasberry Island, a paradise lost to human curiosity far, far within the hidden region of the ocean you call "The Peaceful." For Chris, his own inner wolfishness— whether merely theoretical or no—is a judgment passed, and his doom is sealed; hence no one shall throw his *Fish-loaf* in the fire, because now we must pass on, pass over and on to the dust of Whitlow, where the Perfidian beaded-snake Lord Voljac worshipped hides tittering in the tall grass.

But no, Chris Name is not Van's slayer.

~

Poor Constantine, what can be said for him, done with him? Haunted by the shades of Cioran and Witcacy, his splint is shattered, as he would say. Indeed, he would perhaps be no less at home cradled in my airless embrace, up here, lost amid the endless array of ancient hoodoos, hoodoos oddly like an imbricate in some long ago vandalized Perfidian tabernaculum; one like the fabled

Fastness of Growly Frogs in the Mountains of the Black Worm, where Dionysus the Taborite originated the taboo on all worm-gears and radius gauges, setting back technological development in the Sanjak a good seven-hundred years, at least according to Frank Pierrepont Gielgud, an eminent Englishman who, therefore, ought to know. No, no less at home than down there; than down there with you, on the airless plains of the tri-state, a perpetual Perfidian tumbleweed.

No, no, not even a strict regimen of antitheatrical Interior Positive Imaging (or IPI) prepared in accordance with the precepts of Doctor Truman "Dayglo" Handy at the Ismy County Hospital in New Carthage—along with daily dosages of Doctor Thornley Wolfe's admirable Pepto Bungo—could be counted on to raise him out of his pitiable condition. But capable of murdering our poor Artistic Director Van Rensselaer Board? Hardly. Not unless he had discovered his boss reading the Sufi mystics, or kneeling in what might suspiciously resemble prayer, kneeling in the general direction of Mecca and Medina; and the Mecca and Medina I am referring to is not the twin cities complex along the Animal Fat River, a coarse and unguinous sprawl of malls, horrifically flaming re-agent combines (whose fetid flares still darken the skies for fifty miles about, only to illuminate at night, in an obverse manner, the same haunts, taverns and ditches with wanton pseudopsia, including various ghoul-like things, hobhouchins, both cebo-cephalic and random—illusory of course, but hard on the nerves). Poor Constantine will always be pursued by his native demons (and other Vvilikki), and thus immune to the deep and empty passions of rhetorical New Delbert devilishment or the devilishment of New Delaware and all the rest of it; your land of the flagrant tee-shirt, tee-vee, and your clueless interchangeable theatres, all alike as the profound snores of your seasonal subscribers—a snore that no one who has heard it will ever forget; a snore from deep in the occipital lobe, where the gland determining cultural presence is situated; a snore signifying a deep boredom with all that human life would aspire to, assert and claim for its domain, the domain of the humanly significant.

And as for John Dough$_2$—the less said the better; although the rage of the truly mediocre is a terrible thing, an undying flame dedicated to an empty mausoleum. No, Dough$_2$'s hatred of Van, though pure and dendrophilous in its wily rancor, had long been weakened by the pathetic jactation of the nostalgic has-been —envy, I mean; so that his fury lacked the any-lengthian carefreeness without which serious crime may not be brought to pass. And yet, and yet. Every time I pass over that abandoned meat-locker in Chenango I cannot but feel some compassion for the poor fool. For all over the tri-state area actors are gathering in small, clandestine groups, circles and cliques; in cliques and claques; gathering in a lechery of the performative soul that is the essence of man's urge to prepare; and in especial, the even more unchirognostic impulse to prepare in order to prepare.

Delicate Puella Carpenter presents another contortuplication; her chronic merligoes—or dizziness I think you call it (forever on the move, I simply wouldn't know)—may be related to a certain deep misandry, typical of persons in her position at the better-class of institutional repertory companies; but at bottom it is clear she had a certain fondness for the dear dismembered, at least until the last few moments of his tragic (or is it comedic?) life. Until it became obvious that the Universal Signifier had been up to his olden time devilish tricks; and that Van Board's starling gaze had captured her, just as so many had before. Still, as an enraged bacchante she may well have added her small, white, pierced hand to the general mayhem. Years of humiliation in the dramaturgical anteroom do take their toll, and with all such extreme specializations there is the question of a professional deformation of character; if one may be said to possess such an antiquated and useless psychic appendage—certainly only an awkward and vestigial nuisance in the world of the postmodern not-for-profit. Puella, Dilly, Pooh—Lulu. All those endearing little nicknames, each one a true cut or nick; each one both an unhealing open wound, and an unassailable badge of authentic human propellency. Puella the foudroyant; feeble-forceful, yet forever endearing.

250

And finally one arrives at that demon of reified exclusion, Jackson (Jake) "Burning Spear" Hall, the alpha and omega of high culture politics; the politics of knowing precisely what to say, and what not to say; the politics of shrewdness, and the knee-jerk, the self-congratulatory. Obsessed as he is by the she-wolf of hatred, he might seem a logical candidate as Van's assassin; even if, in all honesty, the she-wolf he sees in (almost) all the faces he derides and dismisses in the fabulous whirligig of his crowded schedule, are the fictions of his own fancy. But Jake loathed Van no more than any other of his kind, the wide river of interchangeable faces of the cowed, the silenced, the intimidated, the pale; for the river of such faces is endless, each one a sad, little moon of insecurity and wishfulthinking. But if the she-wolf Jake sees is truly figured forth in everyone he meets, is it not all the more obvious that the original of all these lies buried deep within Jake himself—a bizarre phalaristic grudge against being, as if the Great Pyramid at Giza had been rotated in four-dimensional space by the wicked magic of Setuthu so as to balance on a single corner of its vast, square base. All sardoodledum, but a sardoodledum not of the deed, but of the word. No, Jake Hall did not murder Van, and I know who did; but first...

27 [A PEIRASTIC VETANDA]:

for all things round are dear to me. For all things round show expansion construed in the erotic, fluid field of empty space. Since I spin about in empty space, empty space is what I am most familiar with. Also, I am such a thing as fills space, and I am good at what I do. For what I do the best is promulgate the lunatic; like the time I led astray the brat of a heiress, Margaret Wolfe Duykinck, causing her to fall for that peccaminous, louche drunkard, John Bayles Fortipton, a failed door-to-door salesman of novelty items who only turned up on the dusty streets of nineteenth century Rome after having been run out of Montpelier County, back east somewhere, tarred and feathered by four brothers of the Monboddo clan, stern upholders of ladies' virtue; along with their three cousins down the road in East Clarence, stalwarts all and renowned oarsmen of unparalleled endurance in the autumn trials at Mount Harum-Scarum College only a few years after its founding by Allan Tacitus Ashbolt, the inventor of laughing gas; alas, the play she wrote about the episode, *Little Sister Death in Big Daddy Shoes* is a real stinker; or, how in the guise of a romantic June moon, I caused poor Howard Stack Movinglow to imagine himself a genius of piano improvisation, so that he made a complete fool of himself, daily, over a period of twenty-seven off-key years, in every concert and recital hall in the tri-state area, at every taverna and nightclub, alienating both family and friends till he put an end to his bitter life by resort to clutching the third rail of the Chenango Metro at the Murray River Street stop near Talking Wand, and was sizzled almost beyond recognition as I glowed numinously behind mountainous gray cloud-castles, sizzled and sizzled as I glowed, all humped up in my cloud-gloomy grumous power and exstacy; or how I maddened pretty Dallas Sumatra, another special person, person of privilege, the debutante and heiress to the Sumatra & Snead Department Store chain and its fortune—with affiliates in Rome, Athens, Sweet Thumb, Drum Head, Golf, Pole Cat, Turkey Lake, Spider Town, Lunchbox, Dimly, Domely, Grob's Attack, Hat

Tree, Robin's Nest, Wiggoo, Flatterer's Gulch, Wingnut, and Suicide's Retreat; poor Dallas, her mind maddened by too much CNN and bible-reading, beheld me one night as the Saviour GogMagog from a far distant world called Stork Shoe. I apparently transmitted a message to her in the form of a pellucid, but very dead, luna moth she discovered on the windowsill, wings glowing in greeny-goldish light, my lustrous light of course; Dallas began to preach a garble of gospels to whomsoever would listen; soon, her strict Presbyterian family checked her into the Sanatorium by Lake Syrtis, Saint Holloway's Home for the Severely Impaired, where the talking cure (reason and reassurance) quickly gave way to the water cure (enemas and forcible duckings), then to the cure of gags, leather straps and severe (and frequent) beatings. The devil within loves to be lashed, lashed, lashed. It is a rule I have witnessed the world round, though a rule that generally must not speak its name. But names, what are names? Hooks and buttons for a flimsy and wholly unnecessary attire. The attire of likelihood, possible-probablies, and the desire nearly all human beings feel to alter facts so that they align with wishfulthinking, and a wishful-thinking always of a distinctly moonish kind, for it is you who have devised the mystery of me, my alleged moonishness. (Am I saying that I am merely another social construction? O madness!) But Dallas Sumatra's fate is like a meal shared with others, so many others it is difficult to keep the whole mad matter in one's mind; it is a syssition of rabid faith-bleeding, faith-bleeding that has commingled strangely with its rabid opposite. For faith's antithesis is also a kind of faith, I suppose.

But no, no, no. I do really wish to be of use to all those who labor, love and sleep under the pale beauty of my almost mythological light. Even though I serve no apparent purpose in the currently sanctioned cosmological order of things it is apparent to me that my reality constitutes a wonder in its own terms. I am truly an apparence, a decorative marvel of apparence. Thus, my philosophy must be more basic even than yours, and more an expression of some higher, self-sufficient clarity. For my true medium is light, undifferentiated dazzle, and what my light reveals is shadow, and the fulfillment of rondure.

To behold me is to behold a species of theater.

To behold me is to witness a physical refutation of that dunce Aristotle; for my liquid motions are as those of any true drama in the unfolding, and yet they possess no beginning, middle or end—not to mention *catastasis,* whatever that may be.

To behold me is to behold oneself beholding me; for all acts of true mindfulness towards the reality of physical presence, all such acts are, in essence, double—for mindfulness itself constitutes an act of worship, and the worshipper worships in the hope of being regarded, re-viewed one might say, by the object of his or her faith (the beloveds); hence mindfulness too might be described as a kind of *performance.* Even in the ancient hieratic churches, centuries after the diatribes of Plato, Origen and Tertullian, the virus of performance runs riot, like a forest fire in the parched Sierras (I have often witnessed this) after a long summer's drought.

What is not seen, is as if it had no being; this is

the peacock's proposition. Be cynosure; that which is ill-framed loses much of her worth. That's the courtier's conclusion.

To behold me is to become aware of the truly sublime; that is to say, there is a kind of drama that is wholly alien to that of the torn tee-shirt, that of the stunning revelation, the stunning revelation that has been so ham-fistedly foreshadowed (how these tedious theatre theoreticians borrow bad tropes from the amazements of my cosmic wimple!) that the revelation usually feels more like an instance of the stunningly obvious, nay, that of the peeling away of outer layers to reveal the deep, intense, psycho-sexual core (what vegetable? What fruit? What magnificent geode can be so clumsily construed?) within; than what is more rare and marvelous, the species of drama that is like stillness and quiet, but is not stillness and quiet; the kind of drama that is about what barely moves, but moves nevertheless; the variety of drama that is always approaching, approaching the inexpressible but never quite arriving at that place, just as the human heart approaches but never quite reaches the place called love, called hate, called home—called anything that mindfulness has somehow brought into narrow focus despite the wailing nightly wind-palaver as it chases an empty can of diet Pepto Bungo rattling across the interstate and clear down the approach ramp just past exit fifty-two at Mink Muscle Creek, where no-one is standing—big, cold Nobody—, no-one on a cold and empty November the first on the far easterly outskirts of mighty Chenango, empire of lights, honks and riddles, empire without a dream other than itself. Big, cold Nobody himself. Empire continually unloading a newer version of itself upon the very site where the previous one has been demolished, broken up (or down) and hauled off piecemeal in an endless succession of thirty cubic yard dumpsters, all this under my moonish and moonly supervision; the place reminding me, even at this boring wicked hour, of another, a few hours down the turnpike as the crow flies, where a corroded meat-locker rests, toppled on its side, forgotten by all. By all, but me.

Still, the devil within loves to be lashed, lashed, lashed; and thus the reputation of the

Great Peripatetic endures, much like the concrete abutments, terraces and blockhouses left over from the last war—the war our unwise people lost (so you say) by following an abnormal and lunatic folly in the form of our late great patriotic leader, now redescribed in all current and corrected histories as the vile, monstrous tyrant he undoubtedly was. Him of the heroic moustachios. The pearl handled, nickel-plated pair of Spiller & Burr automatics and uniform of an odd candy-apple hue so lustrous it seemed like no color found in nature; the heroic him those songs we used to sing were dedicated to, all in outmoded key, played on an out of fashion ocarina, tenor sax, piano forte, and perfectly enormous sousaphone. For the devil within clearly loves a good laugh—at our (your) expense; that and always: to be lashed, lashed, lashed.

Lastly, for the curious among the loony and low, a double definition:

Peirastic, experimental.

Vetanda, forbidden things.

...ends it all on a note of lightness and hilarity. Apparently turning away, one should say instead; for I am fixed in one position for all time, the front of my physiognomy in your face, full and fat in your face, each day the same; become such an object of familiarity as to approach, in the millenarian philosophy of the moonly, the truly strange. To approach, but not quite to touch.

But I suppose in all this mad babble (moon-babble) I have not revealed a great deal about myself, my inner life so to speak; nor have I exposed my ancient psychic wound, and the site of my deep penetralia. Such things always seem, in the estimation of the vast majority of humankind (the FOOLS), to express all the more full and roundy what it truly means to be a member of the human family. As I have mentioned before I express myself most completely in the bulginess of my sheer spherical extension. What lies within might as well be a collection of feathers, yellowing postcards from the days of melancholy, mutton-chopped Paul Hadley Mho, late of New North Devilbus, who devised in 1878 the Mho-mometer, an instrument for the measurement of electro-magnetic conductance, along with acorns, random heteroliths, gravel, sooth-pins, mouse ears and chipmunk tails, bushel bags of neoprene rice collected from under the floorboards of abandoned movie-theaters. But I shall neverthe-less make the attempt to expose what secrets lie most deeply within the cavernous geode of my heart. As, for instance, speaking of furbelows and things of that ilk, I must confess that nothing has caused me to ruminate on the past more than that whiff that reached me not too long ago of...how to described it, my madelaine-Prousty experience? A whiff registered just after the re-cent (and largest in recorded history) recall of hamburger meat from all 45 counties of New Delbert; a recall necessitated by suspected con-tamination at the Triple X Processing Plant in subrural Moonglass (isn't that fortuitous?) by the rare Perfidian trichobezoar, a particularly noi-some furball. This whiff reminded me of the Hot Old Time before the various worlds had coa-

lesced, and all of us spun around trailing clouds
of glory as we flew, clouds of gaseous and semi-
liquid metals; a mixture that would generate
flares and starbursts of such iridescent brilliance
they took your breath away; and also of the concrete site of my oedipal dilemma, and source of
my unbreakable attachment to my harsh, but
beautiful mother, you know who. Mama Terra.
Every time I recall those times I think also of a vision I had, also not too long ago (apparence, not
memory, is my long suit): High above the tree-
line, among the dancing trillium, various sub-
species of the lavish Milwaukee vetch, and other
familiar New Dumbo microflora, a faery ring of
your notables, both classic and contemporary; all
dancing to the lovely strains of Heywood Manly
Thorn's elegant mazurka "madrilene." Among
the happy crew I pick out the philosophers Cermak and Heidegger, Governor Christie Todd
Whitman of New Jersey, the dramaturg Grundschlamm, Riley Dogg Potts, Hugh "Roy" Mann,
Arthur Fit-Hugh Royale, Lydia Yaddo Darkwood and so many, many more; all kicking up
their heels like frisky, yearling colts. And of
course, Perfect Prentiss.

On and on they dance, a circle within a circle within another circle, each smaller and tighter than the last. They are pleased with themselves, and they have reason to be. They have made the world over in their own image; and the image is an arresting one, even if, in purely theatrical terms, it all feels a bit mawkish, a bit micawberish. Mawkish and micawberish at the same time. All this, high above the tree-line on Mount Slanderer's Rebuke, grandest and most sublime (sublimity, the eloquence of nature) of the remote and fearsome Elwood Range, one of the region's certified wonders, and the setting of *My Hole Too Big for God,* the dogged and dizzy runaway hit at New Dumbo's most famous community theatre, The Uncle's Choller Players.

But in truth the deepest secrets I contain do not pertain to the merely human, no, they constitute an immootable and moonly backdrop to the random dither and wiggle of your vainglorious nations, clubs and clans. Your tribes of clams. Some secrets I could pass on that would stop you in your tracks were you able to fathom their implication; but since you are unable to do this, it makes no sense for me even to bother. But there

are some things, somethings of fateful knowledge, bare hints and suggestions of an unusual
and strange tendency, that might crack open the
shimmering egg-like quoz that lies enshrined at
the end of each of your infinite and nearly infinite
regresses. Consider the matter: for I know who
killed Van Rensselaer Board. No one is singularly
responsible (is anyone ever in the American theatre?); the Board killed Board, ripped him limb
from limb like a butchered heifer, or Poland-
China hog. Thus, his death constitutes an unrec-
ognized instance of unpremeditated Boardycide.
Concomitantly, Van Board presents the creepy
occasion of a person suicided (psuedocided?) by a
Board, his own; an example of sardoodledum not
soon to be outdone, surely. A sardoodledum of
the deed, not of the word. If someone asks you
(hoo) (w)hoo told you so, tell them it was me—
you know (w)hoo, the moon. Luna.

~

And as the golden blossom of dazzling goo, of
spongy brightness sends its feathery fingers up

from the remote, far end of the Sweet Thumb river valley, a place so beautiful I had not thought til now there was any human way to ennoble it— a golden blossom spreading out and darkening as the boiling cloud of superheated transuranics, and roughly one cubic mile of New Delbertian loam, phloem and xylem, fur and fingernails, household utensils, paperclips and shoelaces, memos concerning this and that, discarded video monitors, flutophones, tipples, and ocarinas, not to mention all the other commonplace penetralia of the region—vaporized and disintegrated in an instant more beautiful (and frankly more theatrical) than any I have witnessed for quite some time! And I ask you—rises, rippling up, up, and up; the blossoming now darkened through all the deeper registers, reds and purples, as tons of soot and ash rise, pumped fiercely into the upper stratosphere; I ask you to pause and consider. And I foresee a few dark and chilly decades in the tristate area for those who manage to survive. But who (hoo) do mere individuals matter to, after all, in the big picture? Surely a species with such a penchant for cruelty to small animals can appreciate the rich irony in the event, this monumental dropping of the other shoe?

And so another Name is removed, with honor, from the official list; with him go myriad other names, names of the unlucky who made the most monumental of all mistakes, the error of being at the wrong place at the wrong time. An error Heidegger would perhaps have understood, now, had he been able to stand on a craggy perch up here and behold the whole thing, along with longtime denizens like Troilus,Cressida (*this littel spot of erthe*—from Chaucer's version, not the over-rated Bard's), and other names that have come flittering up like injured bugs, like the Scarlet-Tipped Clickety Beetle, crossing the vast, empty blackdress, crossing, crossing, if only to get a brief view of the total picture. To catch a brief awakening and to thrill, perhaps, at the vast and ornamental panorama.

Light delights in light, as does hilarity.

All things subsist in their appropriate revolve. All things apparent or actual, the stuff of apparence. All things flat and all things roundy.

~

It's getting late now, four o'clock in the morning, and I must be on my way (what else can I do?); but let me leave you with another and final perception. Some time ago, again I'll not say when. And I'll not say where—except it was in the run-down neighborhoods of West Palmyra; more precisely, at a humble backyard. A backyard next to the house of a moderately renowned semiotician. Let us call this man Harry Melpomenish, Ph.D. He is a Professor of Theory at Groaner's School for Banausic Dissolves, Theatrical Outflows and Floccify Systems. This man is staring out the window because some children next door are making a racket. These children are named Billy, Josie and Sue. And the little one with fierce, blue eyes: Hannah. These children are playing; these children are making what is called a play, a play that makes no sense.

Mister Harry Melpomenish is writing a book of Critical Theory that, according to his inner clockworkery, floccifies theatrical performance as a symptom of empty cultural drift, a consequence of de-centered hegemony, erasure and a fundamental aporia of Late Capitalism in its final crisis. This man's head is round and bumpy like mine; this man's head hurts. Tenure depends upon this book, a book nearly impossible to write.

Dissolve. Back to the play that makes no sense. A murderous Fluffy Bear has fallen in love with Periwinkle Rabbit and has presented her with a tuzz-muzzy of phlox and gentians (the splendid New Delaware variety which, oddly, resemble the clinging Coleman Morning Glory). Enraged, a jealous (and burgundy velvet) Stedman's Kinkajou, manipulated by fierce Hannah, emerges from an improvised Hollywood bed (a shoebox), and begins a felonious assault—with a purloined rolling pin—on the Fluffy Bear who turns in rage upon him (her); feathers and fur fly and Prince Hamlet delivers a noble speech and to his quietus goeth. Cordelia dies, and Willy and Lear go mad as an angel from Bethesda, Maryland appears before the Kinkajou with a bloody knife. The Fluffy Bear proclaims the importance of being Earnest. Red Skeleton enters followed by a bear, and announces the return of victorious

Agamemnon, a travelling salesman of novelty items; along with Wild Fred, an escaped Christmas tree ornament of indeterminate species. Limbs and branches pop up and out in every direction. No one agrees on how the story is to be told. A light laughter ripples across the rough autumnal grasses, tawny and parched. Sharp shadows perceptibly elongate. Not one of them, the criminal players, looks deeply into the center of things. For them the mystic geode does not exist. All their arboreal narratives overlap, intersect, contradict and merrily counter each other, each to each and each to the other. They are playing, and it makes no sense; and this play is the best play I have ever seen; and this play is called *I Wanna Go to the Monkey Bar.*

Within his gloomy studio, the man turns back to the dark and grainy opacity of his screen. The mystic geode pulses there, unreal. He is deeply unhappy. He will not change his life. There is something the matter with this man. Down the block on Street Road Hill, on Street Road at Leather Mouth Park there is an alleyway. Within the alley are two lovers, pale and gleaming,